PRAISE FOR *LONER*

'A clever, unconventional and hilarious coming-of-age story.'
ELIZA HENRY-JONES

'I loved this razor-sharp, whip-smart, exquisitely funny debut.'
NINA KENWOOD

'Georgina Young's fresh voice and careful writing about
everyday characters made me feel instantly at home.
Read *Loner* and feel seen, feel hope and be entertained—
whatever your age. Young shines.' ALICE BISHOP

'A compassionate and clever story for dropouts and screw-ups.
Georgina Young has bottled the fears and feelings of every young
woman who has had to learn to stop hiding inside herself.'
BRODIE LANCASTER

'Georgina Young made me squirm and swoon and sigh as I fell
head over heels for the exquisite paradoxes of her protagonist.
Lona wonders why she can never say exactly the thing she means—
lucky for us, we have Young, and she articulates all those things
with smarts and humour and grace. This is a book to push into
the hands of everyone you know, especially those who ever had
trouble knowing themselves.' KATE MILDENHALL

'Reading *Loner* was like reading about a younger me:
going to art school, dating the wrong people, living in my
first sharehouse, making questionable hair decisions,
falling out with friends, going to pretentious hipster cafes,
getting lost in Chadstone, waiting for the delayed Pakenham-
line train, experiencing my first love and heartbreak, and
worrying so much about seeming cool and unbothered.
Loner is a convincing snapshot of what it is like to be a
young artist and not know what the hell you want to do
with the rest of your life.' FRANCES CANNON

Georgina Young is a writer and designer from Melbourne. She has previously been published in *Voiceworks* magazine, as well as in *Branches*, an anthology published by the Bowen Street Press. *Loner* is her first novel.

LONER

GEORGINA YOUNG

TEXT PUBLISHING MELBOURNE AUSTRALIA

textpublishing.com.au
textpublishing.co.uk

The Text Publishing Company
Swann House, 22 William Street, Melbourne Victoria 3000, Australia

The Text Publishing Company (UK) Ltd
130 Wood Street, London EC2V 6DL, United Kingdom

Published by The Text Publishing Company, 2020
Reprinted 2020

Book design by Imogen Stubbs
Cover image by Rachel Szopa
Typeset by J&M Typesetting

Printed and bound in Australia by Griffin Press, part of Ovato, an accredited ISO/NZS 14001:2004 Environmental Management System printer

ISBN: 9781922330130 (paperback)
ISBN: 9781925923575 (ebook)

A catalogue record for this book is available from the National Library of Australia

This book is printed on paper certified against the Forest Stewardship Council® Standards. Griffin Press holds FSC chain-of-custody certification SGS-COC-005088. FSC promotes environmentally responsible, socially beneficial and economically viable management of the world's forests.

Dedicated to R. J. Young (1926–2018)

The darkroom

Lona is in the darkroom. She fishes with tongs for her photographic paper, shimmying it slightly so that the developer runs from the surface in small, translucent beads. The inside of her nose itches, tanging with the smell of chemicals. She slides the photograph into the stopbath and rocks the tray gently back and forth for a handful of seconds, before transferring it to the fixer.

The red light on the wall bleeds into the edges of the photographs hanging from a wire line. They are pictures of people, mainly. Tab laughing. Ben loading boxes into the back of a moving van. Grandpa out the front of his house, hands in his pockets. Tab posing with her fingers splayed over her eyes. Tab grinning. The back of Tab's head. Tab with her tongue pressed against her bottom lip. Pictures of Tab, mainly.

Lona lifts the latest image out of the fixer and sinks it into the basin of water. She lets it sit there while she inspects the others. They are snapshots, nothing special. The whole thing (the 35mm film, the darkroom) would reek of affectation if she ever bragged to anyone about it.

She glances at the photo in the water basin. It's of herself: blurry, out of focus. Tab took it, took the camera from Lona and said: your turn. But Tab's used to smartphones and autofocus, she never stops to adjust the lens or the aperture. So this is how Lona records herself, in distorted, underexposed images.

She pokes the photograph with a finger. It sinks beneath

the surface of the water, then rises to breach it again.

'Anyone in there?' someone calls from outside.

Lona tenses. One of the hanging photographs drips.

'Hello?' the someone says.

Lona snatches the photographs down from their pegs, crushing them to her chest. She pulls her film from the enlarger. It isn't until she is pushing her way out of the darkroom that she remembers she's left herself swimming in the water basin.

Out in the corridor she finds Tristan, her old printmaking teacher. Her eyes take a moment to adjust, sensitive even to the dull afternoon light. She squints at him. 'Sorry,' she says. 'Just finishing up.'

Tristan frowns, trying to place her. 'Laura?' he says at last. Close enough to spear a girl through the heart: not quite remembered. 'What are you doing here?' he asks.

She shrugs, the safe answer.

'It's Sunday,' he tells her, an admonishment of some sort. A crinkle digs between his eyebrows. It's coming back to him. Printmaking 101. Lona with hunched shoulders, drawing black rings around her cuticles. 'You don't go here anymore.'

There's nothing Lona can say to that. Her hands are full. She's about to drop her photographs.

Tristan has dark hair that's thinning on top. What's left of it is pulled back into an insignificant tail. He has a wife who is a well-known printmaker. Lona wonders if it cuts him up, being with someone who is better at the thing they both love. If there is a part of him that despises it. Lona couldn't stand being with someone more talented than her.

Tristan smiles at her sympathetically. 'You can't be here.' Which she knows, and he knows she knows, but these things must be said.

'Last time, I promise,' she tells him.

They walk down the corridor together, the soft, worn soles of their shoes barely making a sound. Tristan escorts her to the lift. Keeping her company. Making sure she goes. Either or.

The new lawn

It's been eight months since Lona dropped out. They've finally finished the new lawn.

It's green, wide, flat.

There are ping-pong tables as well. BYO paddles and balls. Other than that, everything's pretty much the same. She walks across campus and there are a bunch of feelings elbowing each other in her chest.

If there's no point in studying art at university, there's even less point in dropping out after a semester and a half. Unqualified *and* spineless. Lona reckons she should put that on a t-shirt. It's not sad if she can stencil it ironically in purple fabric paint.

As a direct result of it being a Sunday afternoon, campus is dead. The cafe Lona used to go to on Wednesdays for coffee is closed. All the cafes are closed. There are a few students in the library. PhD candidates and international students whose sharehouses don't have central heating. Lona can see them at the desks pushed up against the big, glass windows. Laptops and backpacks. Jackets shrugged over the backs of chairs.

It's April, and cool. Lona finally gets around to jamming her photos into her bag and then she's got her hands free to hold in front of her face while she blows on her fingers. It's not necessary, but she enjoys overplaying it: as if this afternoon is something bitter to be suffered through. She's experiencing the pangs of what could've been. What could've been is not necessarily what she wants. But everyone knows that the pangs of what could've been are irrational.

The new lawn is soft and afternoon-dewy beneath her tread. She ignores the signs that tell her to keep off the grass and tramps diagonally across it, cutting a line that's as sharp as she can muster, corner to corner.

Take that, grass.

She gets to the train station just in time to miss her train and so she sits. She plugs her earphones in and pulls up an appropriate soundtrack for the moment. Something with drums like ba-dum-ba-da-bum and a bridge that goes low and slow before it gets really good. She's only got the volume halfway up because she's afraid of going deaf, so it's music stew with all the cawing and beeping and whistling that's going on around her, but what does it matter. The sun's hitting that sweet spot where it's molten amber on the tops of buildings and the girl gives herself a chance to feel all right.

It lasts as long as the song does.

The reason

The reason Lona dropped out of art school was because she didn't like being told what to do with her art—or with anything for that matter. She has hacked off her nose to spite her face so many times there's nothing left of it. She will continue to cut off all appendages if necessary.

Ben's old room

Grandpa moves into Ben's half-empty room. It's been half-empty since last June when Ben took half of his stuff halfway across town to live with his girlfriend in a house half the size.

Ben's single bed looks too small for Grandpa, but Lona doesn't say anything. She makes it up with flannelette sheets and dusts the shelves of the dresser and the cracks on the bookshelf between the books that Ben didn't deem worthy of accompanying him. Kid books and books Lona gave him that he never liked. He always preferred stories about men wandering around post-apocalyptic wastelands and shooting things to those about wizards brandishing magical stones.

The top of the wardrobe is packed tight with toy cars and broken nerf guns Ben used to torment Lona with, but the clothes rail is empty aside from a stack of wire hangers pushed to one end and a leather school jacket that looks like something from *Grease*. Lona can appreciate why he would've left that behind.

She helps Grandpa with his bags. A couple of old suitcases, the kind that buckle over the zip. A couple of boxes full of books that he can't read anymore because his eyesight's gone haywire. Lona starts slotting them between Ben's rejects, just to give her something to do, while Grandpa sits on the edge of the bed looking forlorn.

He's got three copies of *Death on the Nile*.

'You like that one?' Lona asks him, and he shrugs.

She doesn't know what to say when it's just her and him because usually her parents are wheeling around asking them both personal questions that neither wants to answer in the company of the other. Icky subjects like catheter bags and plans for future study. Their relationship hasn't existed much outside of birthdays and Christmases up until now. Just kissed cheeks and blank envelopes with a twenty-dollar bill slipped inside.

Grandpa stares at his suitcases like he's wondering how his life got flayed back to this. Lona stares at the books she's shelving because books are interesting and easy to cope with. The fact is: unpacking them is potentially premature. Mum offered Grandpa Ben's room for the meantime. The meantime insinuates a time outside of the mean. Grandpa knows he's here on good behaviour. Any sign he's going to be more work than Mum can handle and he'll be moved along.

Lona feels a kinship in this predicament.

'Hey, I've got something for you,' she says, and she darts down the hall for a moment. Their rooms are connected at the back of the house by a small hallway. She and Ben used to have conversations from their beds when they were kids and meant to be asleep. Remember whens, they called it. Remember when you always picked Rainbow Road on Mario Kart because you knew I sucked at it. Remember when you made us watch *Cinderella 2* every Friday night. Remember when we broke Dad's favourite mug playing the floor is lava...

This was all prior to Ben becoming a moody teenager who didn't want to play video games with his sister anymore, and the solid few years he refused to acknowledge his association to his oh-so-embarrassing family in public. These days their relationship consists mainly of watching comedies and quoting them over meals in a spitfire had-to-be-there rush that annoys everyone else at the table. Now that he's moved out, Lona has no one to appreciate her shouting lines from *30 Rock* out of context.

She finds what she's looking for on her desk and goes back to Ben's old room. She hands Grandpa the photograph: Grandpa out the front of his house, hands in his pockets. He holds it and doesn't say anything and Lona knows instantly that she's done the wrong thing. Of course he doesn't want to look at the house he's just had to pack up and leave.

Lona took the photo one day a few weeks ago when

the entire family was at Grandpa's, pointing at chairs they wanted to inherit and clearing out the moth-bitten worthless stuff. It's all still sitting there, but it's only a matter of time until Grandpa sells the house and its contents are shoved in the sheds of the various children and children-of-children.

Lona says, 'You want tea, Grandpa?'

He nods. 'Please.'

The big chunk

Tab messages in a flurry of texts. She much prefers the flurry to the big chunk of text. The flurry is in deep synchronicity with her rapid mindfire. She messages:

where are we meeting?

what time?

are we getting dinner?

how much do i owe you for tix?

All four texts are time-stamped 5.39 p.m.

Lona prefers the big chunk response. She likes to agonise over particular words and ensure that she is making herself clear. It is one of Lona's great fears that she is not making herself clear. She never wants anything she says or writes or types or does to be misconstrued. Misconstruction leads to miscommunication and embarrassment.

She messages:

How about Richmond? 7.30? Yes, dinner sounds good (SMILING FACE) anything's good with me. $25—you can just buy me food.

The text is time-stamped 5.54 p.m.

Lona makes sure that she answers every query in a separate sentence in the order that they were fielded so as to avoid confusion. This is messaging etiquette. If more people followed it, the world would be less fucked.

Tab messages:

awesome!!!!

seeee you thereeeee

The band

They're onto their fifth song of the night. It's the favourite of everyone here who hasn't listened to the whole album. Lona is waiting for the second track off their first EP—a completely underrated masterpiece in her opinion. Their new stuff is good, but it's not as crunchy and commanding as the early stuff. Tab recently explained to her that taste is just another name for internalised misogyny. So that smug feeling she gets now, hearing the crowd sing back the lyrics to a song that is too mainstream and not the band's best, is really just a manifestation of self-hatred. Good to know.

Tab's there too, dancing in the dark. Her hair's everywhere like always, desert red and bum long and straight where it likes and kinked where it likes. She grins at Lona, pumps her legs, dances like she's in a Charlie Brown cartoon. Lona sways like there's a rod in her spine. Twitches from the neck, left and right, brain hitting the sides of her skull. When she sings along she's got all the words, knows exactly when the licks curl and the beats kick to life. Lona loves this band more than anything. To her they are The Greatest Band Humanly Possible. She has watched everything they've ever said or sung or done on YouTube.

Even the shaky-cam concert footage.

Even their guest-programmer slot on *Rage*.

They are arguably the sole reason Lona gets up in the morning. This is their only Melbourne show. 'This is so great,' she says to Tab between songs.

Tab agrees. 'This is so great.'

There's a difference between what they're saying, even though the words are the same. When Lona says 'This is so great' she's trying to articulate that she cannot even comprehend this evening and what it means to feel big big love for a concept instead of a thing that has the capacity to love you back. When Tab says 'This is so great' she's saying 'This is so great'.

An unintentional flurry

Despite preferring the big chunk, Lona occasionally opts for the flurry of messages when excited and/or drunk. As the set progresses, she looses several increasingly incoherent messages to Sampson.

Lets do coffee

Coffee tomrrorow

r you free tomorrow?

*tommorrow

coffe tommorrow ok

Tab doesn't ask who Lona is messaging because she probably assumes it's her mother. Lona rarely messages anyone other than her mother. If it's not her mother then she's messaging with Tab, and Tab is currently being told to put her hands in the air and so her fingers are nowhere near her phone.

Tabitha Brooks

Tabitha Brooks is a wild woman. In solidarity with her best friend she has adopted the second track off the band's first EP as her favourite, to Lona's begrudging approval and mild irritation. When the song plays towards the end of the set Tab turns to Lona and grins. Tab is of the belief that friends must share what is most important to them. And moreover, that there is no must about it—friends simply do. Lona does not like to share, particularly with friends. Sharing, when sanctioned, is on the terms of the giver. The terms being:

    a) That Tab may be allowed to like this band, but she cannot like it as much or as fervently as Lona does.

    b) That her opinion cannot be sought above Lona's on the topic when it arises at parties. (It never does.)

Tab doesn't fully understand the extent of Lona's mental arithmetic, the disordered thinking that occupies her mind. Even as she listens to her favourite song Lona is thinking about how she will describe this night later to anyone who asks, how she will insert it into conversation if no one asks, the likelihood of Sampson being here this evening (very low, considering he hadn't heard of this band when Lona mentioned it back in February, he doesn't go out much, he lives five train stations away, stranger things have happened), whether this is even her favourite song anymore, and the fact that it is so hot in here that Tab's hair is glued to her forehead and there are dark, invisible circles under each of Lona's arms.

Tab is having fun.

Encore

The band plays an encore, which is simultaneously infuriating and gratifying. It's not like anyone could see it coming when they walked off stage without playing either of their biggest hits.

Lona gulps down what's left of her now-warm cider and stamps her feet with the rest of the room. One more song. One more song. Her phone vibrates in her pocket and she tugs it out. Stares at the screen.

A message from Sampson.

Shit.

'What's up?' Tab hollers into her ear.

Lona reads the reply. Apparently she's doing coffee tomorrow.

'Sampson,' she shouts.

Tab nods. 'Nerd from uni?'

'Nerd from uni,' Lona confirms.

The nerd from uni is making her insides squelchy. She jams her phone back in her pocket so she doesn't have to think about him and those three simple words: sure sounds good. It's too easy to make it difficult. Or alternatively: *she*'s too difficult to make it easy.

The drummer comes back onto the stage and bangs his sticks together. A one, a two, a one two three four. And here we go again.

The train ride home

There are few things in the world that Lona likes more than the train ride home. It means that the night is over, and however good the night is, Lona is always glad when it's over.

She and Tab sit side by side, Tab's head on Lona's shoulder and Lona's eyes out the window. Tab hums and Lona thinks.

Specs

Lona makes sure she's got her nose in a book when Sampson pulls out the chair opposite. He says hello and she looks up like a woken dreamer—Oh, hi, Sampson—as if she'd forgotten he was even going to be there.

He looks phenomenally undateable. Hair short and blunt cut along his forehead, small wire-framed glasses with one broken arm, David Tennant peering out through the door of the Tardis on his t-shirt.

Lona's loins are instantly ablaze.

'What's up, Specs?' she asks, diving for cover inside the familiar banter.

The name works its usual magic, the blush creeping up the sides of Sampson's cheeks. He grimaces. 'Very little of significance.'

Lona has her thumb in her book, like she's still considering it a viable alternative to the unfolding conversation. She wants him to ask her what she's reading. She wants to know why no one ever asks her what she's reading. It's just about the only thing she wants to talk about and she never gets the chance.

'How are you?' he asks.

This is the most deeply uninteresting question there is. This is the question that no one ever asks genuinely and that no one ever answers honestly. This is a question for people who barely know each other. Lona sighs disappointedly. 'Yeah, all right.'

They get coffee. Lona only ever drinks coffee when other people are. Like a social smoker. She does it because of the itchiness that starts up in her hands when she runs out of things to say to people. She says: let's get coffee. She means: let's do something that enables us to sit opposite each other for a period of time without questioning the point of it all.

Sampson alternately makes her feel giddy and bored. She spends half her time forgetting why she likes him and the other half remembering again. They are woefully incompatible. He looks like he should be smarter than her, but he's not. He studies communication design, but he's doing it for the coding and processing units. They met in Illustration for Narrative, an elective for both of them, during Lona's second, uncompleted semester. Lona had wanted a class outside the self-conscious posturing of the art faculty, and while she adored the unit, he thought it was a waste of time. For the first assessment they had to design a poster for a film or TV series. They both picked *Buffy*, and always sat together after that. Their friendship is seventy per cent talking about television shows.

Sampson gets chocolate foam on the corner of his mouth. It gets beyond the stage that Lona can point it out without it being obvious that she hasn't pointed it out, but has been thinking about pointing it out, for several minutes.

'I miss the caramel slice from that cafe under Building H,' she says wistfully.

'They don't sell it anymore,' he tells her.

She fiddles with her cup and saucer. She has nothing else to say to him. They have run their course. Lona is relieved when he goes.

It takes five minutes for her to start wanting him back.

The real reason

The real reason Lona dropped out of art school was because she liked being told what to do. Being told what to do gave her something to rally against like it actually mattered, and she really just wanted something to matter. But then she realised that she liked being told what to do and it scared her.

Planet Skate

Lona works at Planet Skate on Friday nights and weekends. There are four things she could be doing at any point during any shift. These are:

1) Handling children's shoes and exchanging them for skates that have soaked up the sweat of a hundred feet.

2) Melting cheese onto corn chips in the canteen microwave.

3) Doing loops of the rink to make sure no one's fallen on their bum.

4) Mopping up chunks of corn-chip spew from the bathroom floor.

Lona got the job at Planet Skate because her boss is her mum's best friend. This sort of nepotism is beneficial less for Lona than it is for her mother, who wanted her out of the house. Lona's mother works from home. She got tired of hearing the *Buffy the Vampire Slayer* theme coming from the television five times a day.

Pat is Lona's boss. She is also Lona's godmother. Lona spent a lot of her childhood at Planet Skate, and now it looks like she will be spending a lot of her adulthood there too.

Pat's daughter Jodie also works at Planet Skate. Lona and Jodie have a long, sordid history of Jennifer Lopez dance routines, SingStar, Hama beads and Colin Firth *Pride and Prejudice* marathons. They don't hang out so much anymore because they both realised there were other people out there who have more in common with them

16

than: mothers who are friends. Jodie became someone who was interested in boys. Lona became someone who was interested in pretending not to be interested in boys.

Behind the counter at Planet Skate, Jodie and Lona box step to the Vengaboys. Pat harrumphs and tells them to find something useful to do. Due to the fact that Planet Skate is an almost entirely useless facility, this seems impossible to Lona.

The minute Pat turns her back, Jodie says, 'I've got a date tonight.'

Lona says, 'That's nice.'

'Any chance you could lock up?'

There's no point in Lona pretending to have a life. Jodie has known her long enough to know Lona reserves her Saturday nights for no reservations. 'Whatever,' she shrugs, secretly pleased.

Lona likes locking up because it means she gets the place to herself. She likes the big resounding sound of the silence when the music's been switched off and it's just the smooth roll of her wheels on the worn linoleum. She does laps of the rink, spiralling into the centre, getting closer and closer until she's just spinning on the spot.

At home she knows there'll be Thai takeaway and a debate over which movie to watch on Netflix. Mum will make gin and tonics. Dad will put on the soundtrack to the original West End production of *The Phantom of the Opera*. Grandpa will fall asleep in his chair.

Lona goes skate skate skate until her legs are numb.

Pentax SLR

Lona likes being in other people's rooms when the people aren't there. It's much better than when they are. Grandpa has the photograph she gave him propped up on Ben's old dresser. Pride of place.

Grandpa finds her there, looking. His walker enters the room before he does, dragging his bad leg behind him. 'I found something you might like,' he tells her. He motions to the cardboard box on the floor. Lona crouches to open it. There's a camera on top of the books. An analogue Pentax SLR.

'Cool,' Lona says.

'You can have it,' Grandpa says.

She looks at him, sitting on the seat of his walker, his hands in his pockets, just like they are in the photograph on the dresser: as if hiding those small parts of himself is enough to keep him secure.

'There's a roll of film in here,' she remarks, turning the camera over in her hands. It's in better nick than the old Nikon she got from the Salvos. The film counter is up to nineteen—almost a full roll of pictures, forgotten, probably half-deteriorated in the camera all these years.

'Nothing important,' Grandpa shrugs. 'You can tug it out if you want.'

As if the very prospect of tugging film out of a camera doesn't go against every fibre of Lona's being. 'How long have you had this?' she asks.

Grandpa takes the camera from her and looks at it like

an artefact from another life. 'Got it in eighty-something.'

Lona recalls her mother talking about Grandpa and his cameras: always snapping away, same as you, always fascinated by the latest gadget. He hands Lona the camera back, face blank like he's completely lost interest. He liked it when it was new, when it was symbolic of the future and his ability to shape it. Lona likes the camera for the very opposite reason. She appreciates the staidness of analogue tech, the slowness of it. The necessary deliberateness, because film is finite. She likes using something old for something new, like the act of creation is merely reverb.

'Thanks, Grandpa,' she says, and she feels social conditioning kick in, demanding a kiss on the cheek. But it's just her and Grandpa so she grins instead.

Grandpa almost smiles.

The side fence

In her room she draws the curtains and turns off the light. She rewinds the film and presses the spring release for the back of the camera. She slips the used film into an empty cartridge and puts it in the top drawer of her desk. She's got a couple of spare rolls of black-and-white film, so she loads a new roll and pulls the rapid wind lever.

She used to have a lot of trouble loading cameras. She would take her film into the Michaels shop in the city and spend days wondering how the photos would turn out. Inevitably they'd call her and tell her the film was compromised. On one occasion the film had jammed and she'd taken all 24 photographs on one cell. All the images were superimposed over each other. She had to strain her eyes to see the layered, ghost-like imprints of her mother, Tab, the foreshore at Beaumaris. All of her world a pancake.

She was annoyed with herself back then. She was meant to know instinctively how to do these things. Art wasn't meant to be a thing you had to learn.

Over time she's forgotten those early failures. Now it's easy, instinctive. She opens her curtains and points Grandpa's camera out at the side fence. Increases the aperture with a click click click. She pulls the focus close so that everything melts, then pushes it out again.

There's a big satisfying snap as she presses the shutter release. The shutter closes over the moment as it captures it. This is the first photo Lona always takes, on every camera she's ever owned, to make sure it's working: the side fence. She never trusts the first shot to anything substantial.

She squeezes the lens cap back on.

The real reason
The real reason Lona dropped out of art school was because she felt dead inside every time someone held up a piece of paper with a couple of dots on it and called it art. It was because she looked at what she was making and she realised it was a piece of paper with a couple of dots on it.

Big fat lie

On Thursday night, Lona photographs the year eleven formal at her old high school. She's been doing it since she was a student herself. Back then she did it so she didn't have to feel sucky about not having a date. These days she gets a cool two hundred bucks for the effort.

She roves the function hall, tapping shoulders and asking if people want their picture taken.

'You'll get it back,' she jokes, over and over. No one gets it.

The girls turn instinctively to display their good sides, the boys try to look tough or suave. Both of which are difficult with rampant, take-no-prisoners acne.

She has a small crush on the shorthaired girl wearing a suit and tie who's all arms and legs on the dance floor. She asks Lona if she can take a picture of her, on her lonesome, resting an elbow on a cardboard cut-out of Elvis.

The theme is Old Hollywood. The theme is always Old Hollywood. It has been Old Hollywood since the formal committee held a bake sale to raise money to buy the Elvis cardboard cut-out fifteen years ago.

Lona sneaks off to the kitchen every now and then. Mike the Chef keeps her in champagne. There's a certain delight to being a tipsy adult at an underage event.

She finds Mr Higgins, her old Psych teacher, outside smoking, and accepts a drag, just for the sheer novelty of it.

'What are you up to, Lona?' he asks.

'Shit all,' she replies. She explains the realisation she's had: it's a big fat lie that school is the best it gets for the popular kids. 'It's the best it gets for the nerds,' she says. 'Like, I'm out here in the world and I walk around and no one knows that I'm smart or good at things. It doesn't matter anymore.'

Mr Higgins nods, but Lona can tell he isn't listening. He is twisting his left cufflink around and around, so that the little boat it is shaped like repeatedly capsizes.

Mr Higgins is teacher-attractive. The criteria for teacher-attractive is:

a) under 35
b) not incredibly unattractive

All the girls used to have a crush on him. Lona spent her entire school life expecting him to be one of *those* teachers. The our-love-is-real-not-wrong teachers.

He lights another cigarette and shows Lona photos of his new baby. Lona flicks through the pictures she's taken on her DSLR and Mr Higgins tells her which kids are dickheads.

Roller disco

Since the start of the year, Lona's had to DJ the underage roller discos that Planet Skate puts on every Friday night. Jodie used to do it, but she's since got a life that involves going out with friends and other Friday-night-type things. It was assumed Lona could take up the mantel, considering her known distaste for all Friday-night-type things.

Every Friday she sits up in the raised booth at the far edge of the rink, plugs her ancient hot pink iPod nano into the stereo and plays whatever she wants.

The crowd is almost always identical. Neighbourhood kids plus a few who make their parents trek across town and then ban them from coming inside and embarrassing them in front of their friends. Eleven- and twelve-year-old girls mostly. Trying to work out the things that make them cool. They're gone by the time they reach thirteen, replaced by a new batch.

What they want to listen to, what everyone wants to listen to, is music they can barely remember from their very young years.

Lona plays them songs that their older brothers and sisters and cousins would've bought on CD. Songs they somehow know the lyrics to even if they don't know what they're called. Just for fun, Lona sometimes messes with them. Plays the same song five times in a row.

Owl City on repeat.

The kids love it. They slip over on their skates as they clutch each other's arms and squeal: not again!

Lona talks to the uncoordinated kids clinging to the rail around the edge of the rink. They stagger past her, taking about fifteen minutes for each circuit, pushing their wheeled feet forward fearfully.

'I like your hair,' the timid girls say.

Lona's just redyed it and it's currently radioactively blue. She thinks: just wait. To all the girls who aren't brave enough yet. It's coming. The not giving a fuck.

With the lights pinging off the sad, grimy disco ball, Lona is right in her element. Fleece-lined collar popped on her denim jacket, hot pink Wayfarers from the lost-and-found box. She plays a slow song because she's a sadist who enjoys flinging that awkwardness at the tweens and watching them struggle to slow dance in their skates.

Around 8.50 p.m., Pat waves her arm from behind the canteen counter and taps her watch. Lona leans over the microphone they use for calling out fouls in roller hockey and breaks the inevitable bad news: last song folks.

The kids are hyped up on raspberry lemonade by this point and they wail in dismay. Most Fridays Lona manages to squeeze in four or five last songs before Pat sends her husband Bill over to disconnect the AUX cord.

Parents arrive and kids are pulled by their arms into cars, or if they're anything like Lona was, they struggle to pull their parents away from a car-park gab-session.

Lona chucks her skates on and rolls around the rink with a big, hairy mop, pushing all the plastic cups and chocolate-bar wrappers together. Pat leaves the flashing lights on and it's almost like Lona's some kind of show that people have paid to see. She does a couple of fast laps with the mop swizzling, then a victory circuit with it held over her head.

'Lona,' Pat calls, 'lock up when you're done, all right?'

There's a part of her that wishes someone was waiting for her, elbows on the edge of the rink. Saying things like

24

come on I want to get home and that's it I'm going, even though they'd never, never leave without her.

She slices to a stop and bows. The lights are on and the place is empty. It's just her.

Hold on a second, she calls out to no one. I'm coming.

She swaps her skates for Docs and switches off the lights on the way out. Her bike is chained up outside. She tucks her skates in the basket and kicks off. Home is a ten-minute cycle away.

Sampson's 21st

Sampson has his 21st upstairs at a pub in North Melbourne. Lona brings Tab along as her plus one. Tab is wearing a kaftan. Lona is wearing a denim skirt and an oversized t-shirt with Sick Sad World daubed on it in green fabric paint. She's got two of her jacket buttons done up so it's impossible to read.

'Which one is Sampson?' Tab asks.

Lona points across the room. 'That one.' He's got a blazer on over blue jeans and his face is tomato red with the attention or the five already-consumed beers. Lona waits for him to look up and see her, but he's deep in conversation with someone she doesn't know.

She has bought Sampson a cheap, pointless gift. Season two of *Agents of S.H.I.E.L.D* on DVD. Because it's better than the shit first season, she wrote in the card. He's most likely already seen it and he could've pirated it for free anyhow if he wanted it. Lona wants it to be very clear that she doesn't care and she didn't think it through, even though she spent two months working out how to make it very clear that she doesn't care and didn't think it through.

She leaves the present on a table stacked with bottle bags. If this was a girl party it would be fifty individually wrapped vanilla-scented candles. Lona is not going to have a 21st for this very reason.

'I'm going to get a drink,' Tab says, glancing at the bar.

Lona nods. 'I'll come with you.'

Sampson spots her as she passes, very determinedly not looking in his direction. 'Lona!' he says. 'Hi!' She looks at him like she's been startled out of some very important task—Oh, hi, Sampson—as if she'd forgotten this was even his party.

Then his arms are around her before she can even process how they got there, and he's squeezing like holding her really doesn't intimidate him. She thinks: holy shit. Lifeless arms suddenly squeezing back. It's over before it should be.

She says, 'This is Tab.'

He says, 'Nice to meet you.'

He's drunk, which matters. Lona is not, which also matters. The latter could be easily rectified, but Lona has borrowed her mum's car and is the designated driver for the night. The simple, undeniable maths is:

P-plates = no alcohol = a shit time

Lona has long been known to drive to parties that promise to be massive piss-ups. It's not that she doesn't like a drink. Hell, she'd kill for one now. But she relies on being able to leave when she wants to, when the night's kicked her every which way and she just wants to go home and stew in it.

She'll take the shit time every time, just so long as she's got an exit strategy.

'Happy birthday, Specs,' she says.

'I wish you wouldn't call me that,' Sampson says, brow furrowed, then there's a hand on his shoulder turning him around and there's another person who wants to see him and tell him that they've seen him because that is what birthdays are for.

'Drink,' Tab repeats eagerly, drumming two fingers on Lona's arm, and the bar once again, as always, becomes the horizon.

Black forest cake

Martin introduces himself as Sampson's best friend. Sampson has never mentioned Martin to Lona. She stops herself from telling him this. He explains that he is currently rehearsing for the lead role in a community theatre production of *The Boy from Oz*.

He demonstrates a high kick and sings the first few lines of 'I Go To Rio'.

Lona smiles politely and feels dead inside.

At ten o'clock, someone taps a microphone and the speeches begin. Sampson's father conducts his entire speech with his arm hooked around his son's neck.

He can't believe his boy is a man. He can't believe his boyman has so many beautiful lady friends. Chen, a school friend, talks about *World of Warcraft* and chess club. He too cannot believe that Sampson has so many beautiful lady friends.

Martin grabs the microphone and pulls a two-page script out of his pocket. Looks are shared by people all around the room. Lona enjoys the parts when the jokes fall flat.

Sampson thanks everyone for coming. His mother brings out a cake with sparklers already half fizzed down their stems. The happy birthday song is sung, as is the one about being a jolly good fellow. Chunks of chocolate sponge and cream are handed around on napkins. Sampson cannot bear to face any of his many beautiful lady friends. He stands in the corner with his brother and drinks another five beers.

Lona finds herself trapped amidst the nebulous net of people she used to have classes with at uni. She gets twitchy when she's separated from Tab. She doesn't know who to look at before she opens her mouth. She's pathetic, but she already knows that, so there's no point in telling her.

Her mouth has conversations about typography design and screen-printing and nail polish. Sim says, 'I haven't seen you since Rach's birthday.'

Lona says, 'I wasn't invited to Rach's birthday.'

Rach says, 'I love your boots, Lona.'

Tab materialises beside her, just in time. She puts a hand on Lona's shoulder and insists that this is the best goddamn black forest cake she has ever goddamn eaten in her goddamn life.

Tab likes turning into Holden Caulfield at parties.

Lona introduces everyone and everyone compliments each other's dresses and Tab becomes the centre of everyone's world. It's what she does, what she's always done, sucking the room in like a black hole, except not a black hole, more like a swirling, colourful maelstrom of light.

Martin hovers close to Tab, glancing at the side of her face and nodding when she says things, as if he's testing out what it'd be like to be her boyfriend. Lona presses her lips together and glances over her shoulder to see where Sampson is.

Lona wishes Martin was standing close to her. She wishes anyone was standing close to her. The sound of her former classmates laughing at Tab's stories is skin peeling.

Kings Way

Martin, Sim and Rach jam in the back seat of the Honda, and Lona gives them a lift to the station. Tab flicks through the CDs in the console like she's done a thousand times before, and, like she's done a thousand times before, she settles for the radio.

The car gets hot fast with all of them in it. Martin, Sim and Rach bundle out at Flagstaff, proffering salutes and promising: we'll catch up soon. The word *soon* has been well and truly desecrated by false niceties. Lona understands that it now means something closer to: if we have to.

Tab skims blues and rock and '80s pop on the tuner. Lona drives Kings Way until it becomes Princes Highway and Princes Highway until it becomes Dandenong Road. She revises the night in her head.

Tab says, 'Well, I finally met the nerd from uni.'

Lona considers telling Tab that she is in inexplicable, debilitating love with the nerd from uni. That she has been ever since Sampson first sat down next to her in Illustration for Narrative over a year ago.

She swiftly decides against it.

They drive most of the way not-talking. It's ok because it's them and they have a rule that they don't talk when there's nothing to say. Having nothing to say is all right, contrary to popular belief.

Tab's mellow, no longer the girl at the party with the unwieldy anecdotes and the laugh that hits the ceiling. She presses her thumb to the window over and over, leaving prints that'll make Mum flip. Lona doesn't know what she's thinking. Tab would tell Lona if she was in inexplicable, debilitating love with someone. She'd tell her if she was upset, or if Lona had a bit of spinach in her teeth.

But there are other things. There are always other things.

Things we keep to ourselves.

Sunday night

Grandpa watches all the shows about people in the English countryside peering over each other's fences and being murdered by their reverend's illegitimate son. The television is now almost constantly switched to the ABC.

In the evenings Lona tends to look up from whatever she's reading long enough to see someone get stabbed with a golf trophy or clobbered over the head by the complete works of Shakespeare. Mean old men are constantly being discovered in empty wells after being strangled to death with a violin string, and every second weekend someone tries to open a florist that makes them numerous enemies in the village.

On Sunday night, *Father Brown* is unceremoniously shunted for a documentary about wealthy people struggling to import five hundred kilos of Peruvian pinewood into Wales to convert an old signal tower into an eco-friendly storage-container home.

Lona can tell that Grandpa is quietly devastated.

He switches off the TV and then stares at the blank screen. Mum wheeled his walker over beside the bookshelf before when she was straightening the carpet. He cannot reach it. He is waiting to see how long it takes for someone to notice.

'What are you reading?' he asks Lona.

She is reading a medieval fantasy novel about a courtesan who spends a good portion of the book engaging in sadomasochistic sex. She is not about to tell her grandfather this. She says, 'It's got kings and queens in it. And witches.'

Grandpa nods. He looks sad and Lona can't help feeling it's because his eyesight's shot and he can't read anymore. Lona's caught him a few times now, staring longingly at their bookshelves, which are stacked haphazardly with everything from Kafka to Dan Brown. Mum reckons he used to get through a hundred books a year. Every time Lona shushes her parents when she's reading Mum says: just like your grandfather. It's no wonder he's been attempting to numb his brain on *Midsomer* reruns.

'You want me to read you some?' Lona offers.

Grandpa frowns, as if she's broken some unspoken agreement: never to acknowledge he needs help in any way. She shrugs like it's no big deal and he shrugs back like ok what the hell.

She reads to him from where she's up to. Thankfully the passage contains less fellatio and more political intrigue. The characters all have French names that sound alike, and they are constantly smiling with just the edge of their mouth and muttering wry quips under their breath. Vulgar topics such as bastard sons and trysts are spoken of inside the chambers of the wealthy and there are murmurs of a threat to the monarchy. There are always murmurs of a threat to the monarchy.

Lona glances up and notices Grandpa is back to staring at the blank TV. He clearly couldn't care less if Lord Emmanuel Bernard is outed as an illegitimate heir to the throne before his coronation. She turns a couple of pages and bites her lip. 'Look, the smut is unbelievable, but I don't think you'd appreciate it much...'

Grandpa looks over at this.

'Although erotica is only derided because it's driven by female consumers and authors,' Lona says, parroting Tab. 'Did you know that taste is just internalised misogyny?'

Grandpa sniffs in this small way that is almost a laugh. He's thinking: kids these days. Or maybe just: this kid this day. But he's stopped thinking for a minute about not being able to watch *Father Brown* and not being able to read and not being able to use his leg and not being able to live in the house that he built with his own two hands.

'We've got a couple of Poirot DVDs in the cabinet,' she tells him. 'I can put one on for you, if you'd like. I think we have *Murder on the Links*. I mean, I know it's no *Death on the Nile*, but...'

He nods. 'Thank you.'

She stands up and notices that his walker is by the bookshelf. She moves it back over to the couch where he's sitting.

'Sorry about that,' she says.

Limbo

Pujita from high school is leaving for America in three days. She invites everyone she has ever known to farewell drinks at a bar in town. Tab wants to go because: we may never see her again. This does not overwhelmingly matter to Lona or Lona's general sense of wellbeing, but she agrees to show up at some point after work.

They've got two birthday parties running simultaneously at Planet Skate on Saturday afternoon. One is a group of horrendous eight-year-olds. The other is a group of even more horrendous nine-year-olds. Lona holds sticky hands as she guides tentative skaters around the rink, and she drags orange cones around for the most loathsome of all activities: fun activities.

'Kill me,' she says to Jodie as they stand at either end of a limbo pole.

Jodie shakes her head. 'Nuh uh, otherwise who's gonna kill me?'

Pat has got a *So Fresh: The Hits of Summer 2003 plus the Biggest Hits of 2002* CD on a loop in the stereo. Highlights include:

a) The Ketchup Song

b) Kelly Osbourne covering 'Papa Don't Preach'

Lona's only getting paid to be there until six, but she stays late, as usual. She helps Pat take the rubbish to the dumpsters out back. 'You got anything on tonight?' Pat asks as they heave bursting black garbage bags over their heads into the dumpster. Pat worries for Lona, the way most adults do. They don't like it when children drink and party and have sex, but they are unnerved when children don't drink and party and have sex.

'Yes,' Lona says. 'Dull conversations with people I barely know that make me feel like banging my head against a brick wall. You mind if I do a couple of laps before I leave?'

Pat blinks. 'Just remember to set the alarm this time, all right?'

Like

Lona does a few laps bent over, arms pumping like a speed skater. She clasps her hands together and shakes them in the air like a winner. She gets out the stack of cones and chucks them down in the centre of the rink. Winds through them forwards, then backwards. She pirouettes on one foot like a figure skater. Like a dancer. Like like like. The girl is spinning.

She comes to a stop and she is breathing heavily, sweating. She chucks a sniff under her arm. Right pit smells worse than her left. Always has done. She'll chuck some deodorant on before heading into the city. No big deal.

She starts rolling again without even meaning to. The floor has a very slight tilt. It's a constant source of debate and consternation among the roller hockey teams that play here. Because sometimes just a very small tilt can make a difference, or so the loser always claims.

She does a slow turn. Glides on her skates. The phone starts ringing from behind the front desk. Lona ignores it. A minute later it starts up again.

She can't roll on the foam mats that cover the floor outside of the rink. She has to trudge in her skates, lifting her knees as if she's wading through a Shakespearean river of blood. She gets to the phone just before it rings out for a third time.

'We're closed,' she says.

'Go home,' Tab's voice tells her. 'Get dressed. I'll see you soon.'

Left field

Through sheer will and determination, Lona still manages to be late. She blesses the assorted saints and demons that ensure the Cranbourne/Pakenham train line is almost always experiencing major delays or track works.

At Melbourne Central she stops for sushi and eats it out the front of the State Library. She can see the bar across the street from where she's sitting. She's pretty sure that she can hear Tab's hyena laugh.

She finds them all out on the balcony. She is enveloped suddenly by a sick, sinking sensation that she is back at school. It's not that she didn't like school. Lona preferred school to almost anything that's happened since. It's just something about the way the girls curve their shoulders in to converse in whispered, coded insults. It's the boringness of talking about other people instead of books and television.

In between the it's been so long-ing, her hair gets a good tug. 'Aaaaah, it looks soooo good.'

Lona glances around for Tab. She spots her around the back of the big table, talking to some guy Lona's never seen before. The hyena laugh is getting a good work-out. Lona waves with two fingers. Tab flutters her hand open shut like a clam.

She chooses what she always chooses when she can't get to Tab: the bar. The cheapest white wine on the list. She cannot work out whether saying Sav Blanc or properly pronouncing Sauvignon Blanc is wankier. She spends her entire time in the queue deliberating.

'Saw-vig-non Blank,' she orders, having finally reached a compromise.

It is 8.07 p.m. Lona is begrudgingly willing to give these people one hour and fifty-three minutes of her life, but after that she's outta here.

Back outside, she taps Pujita on the shoulder.

'So glad you could make it!' Pujita says.

'So glad I could come!' Lona says.

Pujita cannot remember enough about Lona to extend the conversation beyond abstract pleasantries. Lona cannot remember why accepting Facebook friend requests used to seem like a good idea. In her opinion, Facebook seems to function for four sole purposes:

1) circulating memes about *The Simpsons*
2) letting you know when people you vaguely know are interested in a vegan food festival
3) facilitating farewell drinks with everyone you've ever met
4) making you feel shit about yourself

Lona finishes her wine and scopes out the least

soul-killing conversation to join. She spies Rowena Cox and makes a beeline for her. Lona and Rowena used to play softball together at school. Lona was left field and Rowena was right. The rest of the team barely tolerated them for being shit at a sport they were forced to play.

'Ahoy,' Lona says.

Rowena has been pretending to message people on her phone. She has actually been making a Spotify playlist tentatively titled: The wish you were at home in bed. It is fifty per cent Nirvana *Unplugged*.

Rowena says, 'Hey, Left Field,' with a grin.

Rowena is studying art at the university where you are meant to study art if you take yourself seriously. Lona studied art at the university where you are meant to study law or science. Lona liked it because no one ever seemed to know that the art department existed, let alone where it was. Their classrooms were part of the old technical college that the university incorporated. They were grimy and dim and full of people handing in artist statements about: what is art.

'But I hated that everyone already had a back-up plan,' she tells Rowena.

Lona has brought Grandpa's Pentax along with her, kitted out with the flash she bought online for her op-shop Nikon. She takes a picture of Rowena baring her teeth at the camera through plum-coloured lips. 'Now one on my phone,' Rowena says, handing over her Samsung. She wants the photo instantly so that she can take it back and say: ew, oh my god, I look gross. Then she'll want another one taken and this one will be just the right amount of growl to look sexy yet fierce for her Tinder profile.

Lona takes a few more analogue shots of people around the table. They look up, blinking, when the flash goes off. They loathe Lona for taking an unprepared moment from them. In any other circumstance she'd feel self-conscious, but behind the viewfinder she feels safe.

Rowena chooses a black-and-white Instagram filter.

Grandpa's camera goes snap snap snap.

The real reason

The real reason Lona dropped out of art school was because the girls still talked about nail polish and *The Bachelor* and all she really wanted in life was to find a place where the girls didn't talk about nail polish and *The Bachelor*.

Teensy bit of wine

The music gets louder and the balcony gets more and more crowded. There is a television mounted on the wall playing a martial arts film on mute. There is a teensy bit of wine left in the bottom of Lona's glass. There, gone.

Lona considers the likelihood of Sampson walking into this very bar at this very moment to greet her with the very words she wants to hear (she doesn't know what these words are, but she will when she hears them). The projected probability is not favourable.

Tab waves Lona over after a bit and introduces her

to the boy she's been talking to. 'Nick went to primary school with Pujita,' she explains.

Nick has a close-cropped beard. He is wearing a beanie despite it being a mild night, so he is either going bald or is a twat. He says, 'Ah, the famous loner.'

'Lon*aaaaa*,' she corrects, even though she doesn't usually bother with anyone else.

There's an empty stool, but she doesn't sit down. She rests an elbow on the sticky tabletop and instantly regrets it.

Tab motions to Grandpa's camera. 'Hey, let's get a photo of us!'

Lona points it at Tab and Nick, gets it so Nick is sliced in half and Tab's waving her hand in front of the lens, mouth open because she's halfway through saying, 'No, one of *all* of us!' The shutter folds over the moment, saves it for later reflection.

Tab rolls her eyes. 'Hold your horses, Lone. Get someone else to take one.'

Lona gives the camera to Rowena and joins Tab and Nick around the back of the table. In a perfect world, it'd be Tab in the middle, an arm around each, but Lona can only get around the table on the side closest to Nick. She hovers at the shoulder of this person she doesn't know and tries to arrange her face in a way that suggests she has no problem with being there.

She can feel the tips of Tab's fingers reaching for her behind Nick's back, reminding her: hey, I'm here.

Rowena says, 'Smile.'

School holidays

School holidays at Planet Skate are their own particular brand of hell. Pat opens every day of the week for the duration. Thankfully the winter break only goes for two weeks, whereas the summer holidays always seem to stretch into eternity. Nonetheless, every day brings with it a new horror.

The kids are younger and the parents skate too, entering the rink on unsteady legs to hold their children upright and inevitably cause massive, collective stacks. At any other time there's usually some semblance of order out there, with kids doing laps all in the same clockwise direction, the more nimble children weaving between the others, tapping their less capable friends on the shoulders as they pass, advising: you've just got to relax. But on school holidays, all bets are off. Chaos reigns.

Tab comes in on the first Wednesday. Tab is a terrible, if eager, skater. She brings her own roller blades, which she's had since she was eleven—the kind of one-size-fits-most blades that click click click out as your feet grow. She's wearing a flowing, witchy skirt that keeps getting caught under everyone's wheels. She waves her hands above her head to S Club 7 and swings a scarf around like Stevie Nicks.

'Get her out of there,' Pat tells Lona. 'She's a hazard to all.'

Lona takes great delight in popping her lanyard whistle in her mouth and letting it screech. She skates over to Tab, sending little kids scattering in all directions. 'Remove yourself from the rink, madam,' she directs. 'Please, before someone gets hurt.'

Tab sticks out her tongue and tries to skate away, but Lona's hot on her heels. She smacks right into Tab, and they both skid into the barrier, Lona's body over Tab's, pressing her into the wall, no escape. 'Listen here, missy,' she says breathlessly. 'We'll have to call your mother if you don't start behaving.'

'Not Linda!' Tab cries, hand pressed to her forehead. 'I'll be grounded for a month.'

They slip, skates sliding out from under them suddenly as they tumble to the floor, all arms and legs. Lona blows her whistle over and over. She feels a hand on her collar: Pat pulling her up by the scruff of her neck.

Someone's just chucked up a heap of Smarties in the boy's toilets. 'And guess who's cleaning it up.'

Proper job

Mum says, 'You need to go back to uni or get a proper job.'

Lona is unsure what qualifies as *proper*. She assumes it means a job that requires her to wear a certain sort of outfit. A uniform, or a dress code. Not just whatever she wants with skates thrown on.

After several thousand hours spent on the family desktop computer filling out applications for frozen yoghurt stores and sending pointless query emails to bookshops that aren't hiring, she gets a job at Coles.

The job requires buying black pants, so she's pretty sure it counts as a proper job. On her first day the manager gives her a second-hand red shirt. It has a nametag already attached to it: Kim.

'We'll get you a new one soon,' the manager tells her.

They don't. Everyone calls her Kim.

She works in the deli. This is a coveted position, apparently. Lona firmly believes that no coveted position should involve handling cold, raw fish. She works with two older women, Janine and Kelly. Jan and Kel. She cannot tell them apart for the first two weeks. She has to wear a hair net, and even though she gets a fresh one every shift, she is constantly convinced she is getting lice. Customers complain when she scratches her head between handling their salami and chicken loaf.

Jan likes to bitch about her ex-husband. Kel likes to bitch about women who bitch about their ex-husbands. Lona likes to nick twiggy sticks when no one's watching.

Unfortunately someone is always watching on CCTV.

Lona is demoted to stacking shelves. 'You're lucky we're keeping you on, Kim,' the manager tells her, before passing her over to a new manager.

There are apparently numerous managers at this particular supermarket. Every second person she meets in store is a manager.

She stacks pasta sauce with Alan in aisle five. He explains that he is manager of aisle five, but Jess is manager

43

of pasta sauce. 'Stick around until the end of August and you never know, you could manage nuts and dried fruit,' he tells her.

Lona finds herself the unwitting protégée of Old Kim. Old Kim says, 'Us Kims have got to stick together.' Lona never questions why this would be the case. Old Kim teaches her how to catch people scanning their capsicums as onions at the self-serve checkout, and how to cut open a cardboard box without slicing any of the packets of mi goreng inside.

Old Kim is the manager of feminine hygiene products. Out back in the staff break room she likes to loudly inform certain female members of staff that Libra Slim Tapered Tampons are on sale this week. 'I know you're a Carefree Super Pads kind of gal,' she tells Cathy—manager of minced beef—and the room at large. 'Might want to stock up while it's two-for-one, darl.'

Lona works five days a week at Coles and still does Friday nights and weekends at Planet Skate. She picks up whatever photography work she can scrounge up and stay awake for.

Mum has been dropping hints about making her pay board. Lona will not pay to live with her parents. She will move out and pay to live with people she likes less than her parents. It's the principle of the thing.

The Coles where she works is just around the corner from home. It is where all the parents of the people she went to primary school with shop. She asks Alan from aisle five to sub for her in the checkout whenever she sees any of them coming. Alan only obliges when he's trying to make Yasmin at the express checkout jealous. Otherwise Lona's left to listen to Kristy Tucker's mother divulge overly intimate details of her life.

'Is that you, Lona? I haven't seen you since the bastard left me for his PT…'

'You must be thinking of someone else.' Lona points to her tag. 'My name is Kim.'

Someone's manager walks past and tells Lona to do up her vest. By now Lona is the manager of checkout number three, so she explains that she's altered the dress code in this particular section of the store.

The other manager, the manager of tinned tomatoes, nods. 'Oh, I didn't realise, sorry.'

No caption

Lona sees on Facebook that Sampson has been tagged in a photo with some girl. He has his arm around her and they both have small, camera-ready smiles, like this is something that has been done before. There is no caption. The girl doing the tagging is different to the girl doing the being inside of his arm.

It could be anywhere, anytime. The photo gets twelve likes. Lona doesn't like it. Lona doesn't like it at all.

The girl inside the arm is called Felicity. She was born on 2 February 1998. She went to Lauriston Grammar. She is a team member at Kmart. She has 458 friends, or at least there are 458 people who were willing to trade an invasion of their privacy for an invasion of hers. She likes *Arrested Development* and Kanye West. She has had red hair since four profile pictures ago, before that she was a soft brown and had braces.

Lona and Felicity have no mutual friends aside from Sampson. Lona and Sampson have eleven mutual friends. Sampson and Felicity have nine mutual friends. Sampson was born on 14 May 1996. He went to Elwood High. He has 326 friends, or at least there are 326 people who were willing to trade an invasion of their privacy for an invasion of his. He likes pages dedicated to *Stargate: Atlantis* and Donald Trump even though he has told Lona on multiple occasions that he hates both of those things. He has looked phenomenally undateable since he first joined Facebook in 2010.

Lona was born on a date not specified on her profile. She went to a school not specified on her profile. She works at Planet Skate, which doesn't even have a Facebook page, and Coles, which she would never pledge allegiance to online or in print. She has 294 friends and she only genuinely likes five of them. She has thirteen previous profile pictures but has never posted anything else.

An hour and some amount of minutes lead to: what does any of this mean.

It means: somewhere, sometime, Sampson had his arm around someone that wasn't Lona.

Shopping trolleys

Tony dropped out of school at fifteen and has been wheeling trolleys around the Coles car park ever since. He wears a *Veronica Mars* t-shirt under his vest every day. This makes him approximately Lona's favourite colleague.

She asks him why no girls get trolley shifts and he shrugs. 'Not strong enough.'

Lona lodges a formal complaint. She attempts to rally other female members of staff. They say, 'We're not strong enough.'

Old Kim is prouder of Lona than she has ever been of her own children. 'Let's take down The Man!' she bellows. 'We'll have a hunger strike if we have to!'

Fortunately it does not come to that. Lona is informed by the end of the day that she can have a trolley shift if she wants it.

When she leaves, Tony offers her a lift home. His car smells like pickles and chewing gum. 'Guess what?' he says excitedly. 'I've just been made manager of checkout number three. Some idiot wanted to switch to trolleys.'

Limp dead leg

Lona gets home from work and the house is in commotion.

'What is this, Bourke Street?' she asks, as Mum runs past with a basin full of soapy water. Dad sprints in the other direction with a dripping, discoloured rag.

'Grandpa,' he says, and Lona feels a squeeze of panic in her chest.

'What happened?' she asks, bag going clunk on the floor of the kitchen as she follows Mum down the back end of the house.

She stops in the door to Ben's old bedroom. Mum's on the floor, sponging at a large red stain. 'Shit,' Lona says. The sight of the blood does something to her stomach. She feels sick.

'What happened?' she asks again, but this time her voice is hardly there.

Dad pushes into the room from behind. Probably neither of them heard her. They are both wearing rubber gloves. The water in the basin is pink brown. Lona realises that this is not the first basin.

She wonders how much blood equates to how many basins. She wonders how much blood equates to significant loss of blood. There is a spiky trail leading from the bed halfway across the carpet. It ends, so if it ends, the bleeding must have ended. If the bleeding ended, then that means one of two things. Mum not-speaking, sponging on the floor means one thing.

Lona hears her name called from the other room. She hurries into the bathroom and finds him sitting on his walker, a large padded patch on his leg. Grandpa is grimacing. 'I thought I heard you get home,' he says.

'What happened?' Lona asks. There's a big bruise of blood through the gauze. The skin around the patch is purple and blue. There's no muscle in his legs, not since the right one lost all feeling. His skin is like crepe paper.

'Ah, just caught my leg on the bed post,' he says, resigned. 'Made a spectacular mess. I'm fine.'

Lona nods. All that blood from that limp, dead leg.

'I'm fine,' Grandpa says again.

Clean undies

Lona gets her period. It arrives with a vengeance. She wakes in the morning soaked through her undies. The insides of her thighs are smeared with it. She gets up blearily and stumbles into the bathroom with a clean pair of undies and something to jam inside of herself to make it stop.

Like always it's arrived when it wants to, this time a week and a half before she expected. She wonders: can she be a proud, strong woman if this innately woman thing makes her feel neither proud nor strong.

In the laundry sink she rinses out the blood, lets it run diluted down the drain. Mum finds her there and says: keep the tap running.

Lona leaves her underwear to soak in the yellow plastic basin that was yesterday full of pink soapy water. She gets ready for work.

Phone screen

Tab's phone screen lights up and so does her face. She's messaging with Nick again.

Lona tries to focus on the film they're watching. It's a psychological thriller about a woman whose split personality may or may not have killed her husband's lover. Lona is exhausted from work, and her eyes hurt from straining to see what Tab is typing.

Tab laughs.

'What?' Lona demands.

Tab points at the television. 'Cop with the pornstache is back on the case. I thought you said this was meant to be a good movie?'

Lona rubs her eyes. 'I said I'd heard of it, I didn't say it was meant to be good.'

Tab puts down her phone and pauses the film. 'Hey, what's up?'

The question makes Lona's hackles rise, like always. As if any enquiry into her state of mind is an accusation. She presses her lips together tightly. 'Nothing.' It's been a while since Tab dated anyone, since she's even been interested in dating anyone. And back then it was always just someone they both knew from school, some boy or girl who'd be around a bit and then wouldn't be. Lona had other things to do then: trigonometry, art projects, slog through set texts.

But it's been almost two years since they graduated. Something has happened to Lona since then. Tab's not just her friend anymore, not just her best friend. She's the only person Lona ever wants to see, the only person Lona thinks will ever want to see her.

She takes the remote and unpauses the movie. 'I'm fine,' she says. 'Really.'

Bombed out

Lona realises she hasn't seen Tab in two weeks. Usually it's Tab who contacts Lona when it's been this long. Lona has a tendency to go for extended periods of time before realising she can't remember the last time she interacted with another human being. Tab's usually the one who jolts her out of it. This time, it's a lack of Tab that does it.

Lona much prefers being the contacted than the contacter. Being the contacted means feeling wanted, whereas there is always an inherent neediness and self-consciousness to being the contacter. Even with Tab.

She finds herself irritated with Tab for putting her though this. Tab knows how she feels about these things. At least, she thinks she does. It's not like they've ever talked about it. It's not like Lona has ever said: this is how I feel. Or even: I appreciate it when you call. These are the things she thinks are implied. These are the things she wants Tab to know instinctively, even when Lona struggles to articulate them.

She sends a message. A big chunk:

Hey, how have you been? Are you free tonight? Coffee in Oakleigh?

Three times question mark, three times hesitation. Tab messages back straight away as if there's not been all this time and metaphorical, existentially examined space between them:

i'm bombed out after uni

sorry

Lona endures this first knockback gracefully. She replies:

Do you want to go to the Winter Night Market at the Queen Vic on Wednesday? (CLINKING BEER MUGS) (STEAMING BOWL)

Tab says:

woulda loved to lone but i'm going out with nick!!

Tab uses exclamation marks to convey a wide variety of emotions. Here, Lona assumes, she's going for regret or excitement. Potentially both. At that exact moment, Lona decides that people spend way too much time on their phones. She turns hers off and throws it in her bag.

The double date

Despite not registering for a seminar on Nick's Personality And Life, Lona finds herself attending one when she finally manages to pin Tab down for afternoon tea. They sit on the floor of Tab's bedroom like they always have, a plate of Tiny Teddies on the carpet between them. There are scarves hanging from and draped over every possible surface. The entire front of the wardrobe is covered with pictures of women reading books or holding random objects (pot plants, kitchen utensils, a lampshade) over their faces. As Lona fidgets and switches from cross-legged to legs-stretched a hundred times back and forth, she learns that Nick is a fan of the double date. From what Tab says, Lona would go so far as to describe him as an avid disciple of the double date.

Tab tells her that's she's already been out with Sam&
Dan and Anna&Beth and Jules&Hugh. She talks about
Nick's friends in pairs, like their names and extremities
are stuck together with hot glue. Like they are some sort
of unfinished craft project Lona has thrown back into her
drawer, bits of string and wool and balsa wood entangled,
never to be restored to whole parts.

They are always Nick's friends. Nick apparently has an
endless supply of happy, loved-up friends. Tab and Lona
have no happy, loved-up friends. 'They're all virgins or
weirdos,' Tab says, shrugging, and Lona can only nod.

As both a virgin and a weirdo, Lona can rest assured,
knowing she will never find herself participating in one
of Nick's double dates. According to Tab, she misses
out on a fun-filled evening of dinner&movie. Dinner is
almost always Asian fusion, the movie is almost always
forgettable.

'I thought double dates were meant to be for when
a couple gets bored of talking to each other,' Lona says,
irritated they have gotten through a whole box of Tiny
Teddies without discussing a single book.

Tab laughs. 'Well, what can I say? Nick and me have
hit dire straits early on.'

She's joking, unfortunately.

Moving out
Lona moves out with Sim and Rach from uni. They get a
two-bedroom house in Carnegie. Lona is paying slightly

less rent than the others. She sleeps behind a curtain pulled across half of the living room.

She has brought all her books with her, but very little else. She uses stacks of them as furniture. She spills tea all over her original-cover-design Harry Potter collection. She calls Tab in tears: her childhood is ruined.

Tab takes her extremely seriously. They talk until 1 a.m., Lona's phone pressed close to her head even though she's afraid of getting brain cancer.

'This was a colossal mistake,' she says.

'What was?' Tab asks.

Lona doesn't have a short enough answer. So she says, *Goblet of Fire* is almost dry.'

'You good, Lone?'

She stares at the ceiling. 'Yeah, pretty much. Night, Tab.'

'Night.'

The house is quiet because Sim is out and Rach went to bed early so she can get up to jog and eat granola in the morning. Lona has her reading lamp and her single bed and every book she's ever owned except for the ones about horses and unicorns that she left behind at home. The curtain dividing her space from communal space is just a sheet pegged to a piece of string.

Rach said: just for now.

Lona liked that because that's exactly how she feels. The dropping out and the Coles and the moving in with almost-strangers and the sheet pegged to a piece of string: just for now.

Despite her understanding of the infinite nature of now, Lona has her hopes.

The rites of passage

It was never decided that there would be a party. It was simply assumed. When Sim asks them, 'Friday or Saturday?' they both know what she is talking about. The proposition that there are no rules to growing up is inherently wrong. There are many. The rules and the expectations are known, even if they are various and contradictory. New house equals a warming of said house. These are the rites of passage. You shall not pass until your house is hot with the breath of people you used to be friends with and can't remember anymore why you liked. Lona suggests not-Friday because she has to get up early on Saturday morning for work.

'Friday,' Rach says definitively. It's definitive even though it's offered like a suggestion. Lona knows she will not win with Rach. She knows she will continue to know this. Living not-alone feels lonelier than it should. She does not know why anyone would live not-alone if they could live alone.

Lona cannot live alone, not even with three jobs. Not even when she works early on Saturday mornings. Her money, stood at checkouts for, smiled at strangers for, stared through lenses for, bored to death for, is not enough to live alone in a one-bedroom flat. Lona wants to know what the rules are, the rules to being an adult. But she's heard them, seen them embodied and avowed a hundred ways on television shows about twenty-somethings who drink too much on weeknights and never wear the same outfit twice. She's rolled her eyes at them.

She doesn't want anyone to tell her how to live. She's begging for someone to tell her how to live.

Semiotics

Tab sits on the bed while Lona dabs purple lipstick onto her bottom lip.

'You kidding me?' Tab says. 'You brought your single bed with you? It's time to upgrade, Lone. Come on, what's a boy going to think?'

'What boy?'

Lona is not being facetious, but she is perhaps being hopeful. Sampson, she wonders senselessly. Or maybe there is some boy she isn't yet aware of. Some boy who has been whispering to Tab about her, some boy who would be thinking about her bed, single or not. These thoughts are shallow dishes, the kind that wipe clean immediately.

Tab is wearing jeans with flowers embroidered on them. Red flowers with green leaves. This is the basic flower. These are the roses held between the teeth of lovers who tango. This is the basic format of love. Red flowers with green leaves can be stamped on anything and the connotation is clear because of the semiotics. Lona learned about semiotics at university. She learned about love watching movies and staring at the legs of her friend.

'When's everyone getting here?' Tab asks.

Lona shrugs, but the shrug is rendered redundant even as it is enacted because she answers, 'Eight. I'm tired.'

'You're always tired,' Tab says.

Lona presses her lips together. It looks like a ballpoint pen leaked in her mouth. 'So?' she says.

Warming the house

The block is big but their house is small: old carpet, picture rails, speckles of mildew where bookshelves have sat against walls, sliding doors with yellow glass panels. Three art makers in a confined space so there are pictures, paintings, projects everywhere.

Lona manoeuvres her way into the kitchen. There's a big plastic bowl filled with pesto pasta on the counter. Sim made it earlier for god knows what reason. No one eats pesto pasta before a party. They only have two cereal bowls and they're grotty, so Lona opts for a mug. She spoons some farfalle into it.

A girl she doesn't know pulls a bottle of white wine out of the fridge and says, 'What's that? Pasta or something?'

Lona nods and chews.

'What have you been up to?' the girl asks, almost like they're meant to be friends or something. Lona squints at her and realises they probably are, or they were at any rate. Her name is Liv, Lona thinks. Liv used to talk to the people Lona talked to at uni. Doesn't make them friends, but it does make them people who have to ask each other inane questions when they find themselves in a kitchen together.

'Work mainly,' Lona says.

Liv nods and sips from the glass she's just poured. 'Nice place,' she says.

Lona shrugs a: yes and no. 'I sleep behind a sheet pegged to a piece of string,' she says. 'I am too self-conscious to masturbate.'

Liv leaves her alone.

Empty plastic cup

Tab finds Lona in a corner, about *this* close to getting out a book to read. There's lipstick bruised on the rim of Lona's empty plastic cup.

'I don't know anyone here,' she says. 'How do I not know anyone here?'

Tab pinches Lona's shoulder. 'I want you to meet someone.'

'Who?'

'George, get over here!'

A figure across the room turns and looks in their direction.

He is tall, dark-haired. Thick-framed glasses like Clark Kent. Tab says, 'Lona, this is George. George, this is Lona.'

Lona looks up at him from the armchair and knows that Tab will be hoping that she will find George both interesting and attractive. She thinks about how unlikely it is that she will ever find someone both interesting and attractive. She says, 'Hi.'

'You're the best friend,' he says.

She, the best friend, nods. 'I suppose.'

George likes that she uses the word *suppose*. She can tell, can see something shift in the way he holds his mouth.

'This is your party,' he says.

Lona looks at Tab. Raised eyebrow a question: does he always speak in statements?

'George is studying medicine,' Tab says, with a wicked smile. 'Lona's a dropout with minimal prospects.'

Back in a sec

George is studying music as well as medicine. 'Interesting combination,' Lona says. Due to her significant lack of flirting game, Lona tends instead to engage in actual, intellectual conversation with prospective fuck buddies. She does abnormal things like get to know them and attempt to gauge what their politics are around victim blaming.

'Neither was my choice,' George says.

'Oh yeah?' she says, not entirely certain yet whether she is actually interested in anything he has to say.

'I'm going to be a cardiologist. I was always going to be a cardiologist. Oldest son equals the responsible one, you know? I'm neither happy nor unhappy about it, if that makes sense. Cello was about discipline. Mum took me to my first lesson when I was six. I like it in a very Stockholm syndromey way, if that makes sense.'

George likes the phrase: if that makes sense. Either that, or he thinks Lona is an idiot who cannot make sense of anything. He is potentially nervous. Lona is potentially making him nervous.

'Rape culture,' she says. 'Yay or nay?'

George stares at her, head tilted slightly. 'What?'

He has pulled a chair over to sit next to her. This is the most proactive thing someone has done to talk to her in years. Tab keeps sending thumbs up from across the room. 'How long have you known Tab?' Lona asks.

'Not very long. I really only know her through Nick.'

That makes sense. George is clearly from the Nick oeuvre.

'She said I should come tonight. I don't usually turn up to parties I wasn't invited to. I just thought I should do something different for once, if that makes sense—shit, I've said that like fifty times haven't I?'

Lona shrugs. 'Well, you haven't not said it like fifty times, if that makes sense.'

It takes him a moment to realise she's messing with him, and then he laughs. His hair is straight, black, jaw length. His smile is warm and genuine. She finds herself grinning back. He gets up for another drink, the last can is empty and useless in his hand.

'Back in a sec,' he says.

Not coming back

Back in a sec turns into not coming back. Lona waits in her armchair but he's obviously found something more interesting up the other end of the house. It shouldn't make her feel shit, but it does.

She retreats behind her curtain. Lies on her bed and jengas a book out of one of the stacks by her mattress. *Finnikin of the Rock*. An old favourite, but she's so careful with it that it looks like it's brand new. She can't read it over the music. Her head hurts. Everything makes her head hurt. The twinge of the curtain and it being pulled back by George makes her head hurt. The embarrassment and his 'Sorry' at finding her horizontal makes her head hurt.

'Um,' she says, aware that from the angle George is looking at her, she would appear to have approximately five more chins than usual.

'I'm sorry,' he says again. He has brought her a can of hard cider. Back in a sec apparently meant back in 1200 secs. She sits up, finds herself saying, 'I'm not feeling well, sorry.'

They throw sorries back and forth. Lona is on the cusp of saying something stupid like: actually, why don't you stay, I'm not actually sick, I'm just sick of everyone else out there. But it isn't true and her head is pounding and she offers all she's capable of: it was nice to meet you.

'Yeah,' he says, like he's still on the fence. He nods and goes.

Lona collapses back onto her single bed with a groan. She kneads her head and hates herself, but neither activity achieves anything, so she just stares at the ceiling until everyone leaves. Tab finds her later and squishes onto the bed beside her and says, 'I'm amazed you lasted as long as you did.'

If this was an American indie movie, they'd sleep together like spoons in a tidy drawer. But this is a sharehouse in Carnegie and she is a girl who brought her single bed with her when she moved out because she wanted to make it clear that she never has and never will need anyone else.

Tab sleeps on the couch. Lona sleeps lightly and unsatisfactorily.

Grandpa's birthday

Mum makes an orange cake for Grandpa's birthday. They have a picnic down by the beach at Ricketts Point. Lona brings tzatziki. Ben brings an excuse as to why he's 45 minutes late.

He and Lona sit together at the end of the table and tell each other amusing things that have happened when the other wasn't there. They reach over each other without asking to get food, and debate which composite of *Friends* characters everyone at the table is. 'Mum's a full Monica,' Ben says. 'Dad's like some kind of Phoebe-Joey.'

'Has appeared in amateur theatre, loves singing in public,' Lona agrees.

'You think you're a Chandler, but you're a Monica-Phoebe. Offbeat, but anal as.'

She crosses her arms. 'Well, you're a Ross.'

Ben looks stricken. 'That's just hurtful.'

Up the other end of the table, Mum talks about her childhood and the grandmother Lona never knew. Aunty Jas is there, and Cousin Rob. Grandpa unwraps his presents. Long socks and a pair of elastic-waisted shorts. Lona gives him her gift. An audio book CD. It's the novel that everyone's talking about and reading on planes: a murder-suicide gone wrong in the outback. Grandpa turns the plastic case over and looks at Lona quizzically.

'I'll help you set it up next time I'm round,' she says.

The next time Lona is round is two days later. She calls in at home to pick up her DVD of *10 Things I Hate About You*. This is a thinly veiled excuse to enable her to lie on her parents' couch and wish she were more motivated in life.

She gets her old CD/cassette/radio stereo out of the back shed and connects it up in Ben's old room for Grandpa. 'Now you just put the CD in and press play,' she tells him. He does not look overly enthusiastic.

The photograph of him standing out the front of his house is still on the dresser. There are two polaroids beside it: one that Grandpa took of Lona and one that Lona took of Mum.

Grandpa presses play on the stereo after much cajoling from Lona. They listen to the first few lines. Lona keeps an eager expression frozen on her face. Grandpa says, 'Thanks Lona,' and presses stop.

'Oh no!' she cries. 'You've got to press pause otherwise it'll go back to the start.'

'Hm,' Grandpa says. 'I see.'

Lona makes them both tea and then Grandpa takes a nap. She tells him to call her if he has any difficulties with the CD player. She takes *10 Things I Hate About You* and *She's the Man* and *Clueless* from the DVD cabinet. Anything that takes a revered work of literature and stuffs it into high school melodrama. Mum says, 'Come for dinner Friday.'

Lona says, 'I work Fridays. I always work Fridays. Have you forgotten everything about me already?'

Mum rolls her eyes and doesn't ask her to stay for the bolognese that is currently bubbling away on the stovetop. Lona has got to refine her technique.

Prosciutto-wrapped melon

Lona photographs Alan's sister's 18th birthday party. There are a lot of people in Alan's parents' house. More people than Lona can comprehend knowing or liking. Alan's parents are apparently loaded. They make him work at Coles for the sole purpose of building his character. Lona is getting paid more for the gig than she ever would have asked for. The house is beautiful. An old brick mansion in Malvern East.

Lona chews on prosciutto-wrapped melon between shots.

Alan's little sister Tilly pulls her around by the wrist because she needs to have a photo with everyone while her make-up is good, otherwise what's the point in even throwing a party.

The music is loud and peppily misogynistic. The guests are drunk before they arrive. Everyone is equal parts afraid and in reverence of the camera. They want to see their photo before it is uploaded to Facebook in an album titled: 18 (SPARKLING HEART). They prod their greasy prosciutto fingers against the display screen as Lona shows them and they say: can you zoom in just a bit. This is the fear of being caught for one moment in a position that was not properly manufactured for mass consumption. This is the fear of representation of self subsuming the self.

Lona is not using a wide-angle lens. This is inexplicably disappointing to some. These young people are used to a wide-angle lens. They want the shots that they get in nightclubs that always make at least one person on the edge of the frame look like a misshapen leprechaun.

'But you will put a blue filter on it, right?' they ask desperately.

Lona tells them whatever she thinks will help them sleep at night.

At around nine o'clock she notices there's someone looking at her from across the room. He waves. It's George. He comes over and there is the usual tennis match of what are you doing heres that the situation requires.

George tutors Tilly in Maths Methods. Her mother

insisted he come along, he explains to Lona's bewildered expression.

'I'm really just here for the fancy cantaloupe,' he says. 'Eighteen-year-olds are exhausting.' He has his hair pulled back into a short, blunt bunch. He is wearing a loose tie. He looks nice.

'You want a picture?' she asks. He doesn't know how to pose. He just stands. Lona smiles with her face squashed behind the camera.

He follows her around as she takes photographs. The faces that present themselves to her get sweatier and blanker. She caps the lens. No one's going to appreciate any documentation of the night from this point onwards. Time for the party to belong to itself.

'You want a drink?' George asks. She experiences a momentary flashback cringe to the hard cider, five chins incident. He gets her a glass of moscato.

'I didn't realise your opinion of me was so low.' She grins, gulping thirstily at it.

'Classic white girl, classic white girl drink.' He grins back.

They sit on the nice couch in the nice front room that has all the nice furniture in it. They are exhausted because they are two years older than everyone else here and it is their solemn duty to sigh: I'm so glad I'm past that.

They talk books. George tells her that he's reading Gogol, because he's trying to impress her with something literary and obscure. She tells him that she's reading *The*

Hunger Games because she's trying to impress him with something so mainstream and prolific it's practically post-modern.

He plays bass in a funk ska band. He looks so nice.

Lona is folding herself into the possibility of his mouth on her mouth and she's aching like her body actually expects her to go through with it.

Alan's mum hands Lona an envelope chock-full of rich-people pay and Lona waves it at George: midnight pancakes? Macca's? The words almost exist. She taps the corner of the envelope on her silent lips. George looks at his watch. 'I should get the train,' he says.

'Oh, right,' Lona says.

The hug is firm, friendly. 'It was good to see you, Lona.' She nods. 'Yeah.'

Nick

Occasionally, as is statistically likely, Lona and Nick are left alone in each other's company. This occurs when Tab:

a) goes to the bathroom
b) takes a phone call from her parents
c) insists it's her turn to make tea
d) runs into the next room for that book she wanted to show Lona

Whatever conversation they were having with Tab inevitably peters out with a forced laugh from either party, and then they are left to fend for themselves. Lona slips into the little-researched gap between fight and flight that involves going rigid and staring straight ahead. Nick thumbs at his phone like he's the kind of person who would be getting a whole lot of messages at 10.30 p.m. on a Thursday night.

Sometimes he will try to start a whole new conversation. Lona does her best not to look at him in disbelieving horror. Surely he knows that Tab is the only small, tenuous thread that keeps them swinging around in the same orbit.

'You follow the footy?' he asks on one occasion. They are at a sports-themed pizza bar in Hawthorn. Tab has just gone to order drinks. There is a life-size picture of LeBron James on the wall. There are multiple television screens displaying multiple different combinations of men throwing around balls.

'No,' Lona says.

Despite the negatory response, this *is* Melbourne, so the follow-up question is inevitable either way. 'You have a team, though?'

Lona sighs. 'I have a problem with the fact that two of our state public holidays are dedicated to sporting events which encourage excessive gambling and glorify talents that contribute nothing to society as a whole.'

Nick blinks. If he was faster or meaner, he might point out that art contributes nothing to society as a whole, and neither does making smartarse comments about things. But he just smiles and shrugs. 'Got me there.'

Nick is potentially attractive, but seeing as he has clearly belonged to Tab since the first time they met, Lona sees him less as an actual man than: the person that Tab is seeing. He is going bald, or at least he will be in a few years' time. He's got what's left of his hair shaved close to his skull. Everywhere else he's dark, thick fur. Eyebrows, eyelashes, beard, forearms where he's got his shirt rolled up. He's studying law but he never talks about it. He loves Tame Impala and Murakami, both of which he always talks about.

He lent Lona his copy of *Kakfa on the Shore* two weeks ago. He says it's his favourite book and that he's read it five times, which is clearly evident. The cover has been bent back so much it's held together with tape. It is the complete opposite of the straight, perfect paperbacks that fit in Lona's alphabetised stacks. She told Nick he was guilty of book abuse. He told her he doesn't trust people who are afraid to crack the spines of the things they love.

Nick is trying to be her friend. She realises this, but she also resents it. She doesn't want to have to be friends with someone just because Tab is enjoying their coital and intellectual company. She never wants to do anything just because. Just because is a stupid excuse for pointless life decisions.

Tab returns to the table with a jug of cider. 'Drink up, kidlets,' she says. 'Movie starts in twenty minutes.'

They are going to the Lido to see a film that Lona doesn't really want to see, but they couldn't get tickets for the one Tab suggested first and hey, Nick says this one is meant to be really good.

The upside: at least if it sucks, Lona can hold it against him for the rest of her earthly days.

Burgers

Tab does exactly what Lona secretly wants her to do but is too afraid to ask, lest it become obvious to anyone, ever, that Lona Wallace has feelings that can be hurt and unfulfilled and used against her. Tab organises a double date with Nick and George.

'Jesus, I'm not a charity case,' Lona says, scowling. The moment Tab leaves the room, Lona punches the air like she's in the fucking *Breakfast Club*.

They go out for burgers in a warehouse restaurant in Moorabbin. Lona has seen herself eat a burger once when she was seated opposite a mirrored wall panel at Grill'd. 'Really?' she questions Tab, who has had to endure the sight of Lona wolfing a burger on numerous occasions herself.

'Get it out of the way,' she shrugs. 'If he wants you after this, nothing's going to put him off.'

Lona and George sit next to each other so that she gets the press of his elbow through her denim jacket. Tab has engineered it this way. Lona doesn't know why. She likes having a table between herself and any other human. It feels too unnecessarily intimate to turn to speak to him when he is right there.

She solves this dilemma by staring down at her food while tomato jam and patty grease trickle through her fingers. She doesn't look at anyone aside from Tab, who keeps giving spasmodic head jerks in George's direction. Lona barely says anything. She feels stupid and uninteresting. She wants to dig something out from between her front teeth but she is unsure if this is something you can do in front of the person you are futilely attempting to imagine yourself being with.

Afterwards Tab drives Lona home. 'You should have told me you didn't like him,' she says. 'He's into you and tonight would've been pretty sucky for him.'

Lona allows herself to be chastised. She goes home and lies awake, her fingers finding the places she wishes she was brave enough to let him touch.

Full trolley

Lona buys a pair of fingerless gloves, the kind you get if you ride a bike a lot. She veers around the car park at Coles with stacks of trolleys, blisters blooming on her palms regardless.

Trolley duty is shit. But because she negotiated for it as a feminist statement, there is no way she's giving in.

She spends hours jamming trolleys that fit together, and unjamming trolleys that don't fit together. She rescues strays from the grass out the front of the store over and over again. She loses all faith in humanity as a species. Her hypothesis: people are shit and lazy, and their treatment of shopping trolleys is symptomatic of this.

No one looks at her anymore. She is a trolley wheeler. A leper. She finds herself muttering under her breath, curses

71

and snide remarks. Legend grows about the crazy lady who haunts the Huntingdale Coles trolley depositories. Mothers yank their children away from her. She no longer gets any counter shifts. She has gone full trolley.

Even Tony no longer meets her eye. These days he actually buttons his vest over his *Veronica Mars* t-shirt. Now Duncan is the only visible character. This is perhaps the greatest tragedy of all.

Lona wonders if her spirit is being crushed.

Home for dinner

On Sunday night, Lona goes home for dinner. Mum makes a roast and Ben brings his girlfriend. Dad and Grandpa are at either end of the table due to the patriarchal structure of society. Lona is dumped over against the back wall with Harriet.

Lona does not know if she likes Harriet. She doesn't particularly not like Harriet, it's just that Harriet has never made an attempt to be anything other than: girlfriend of Ben. Harriet asks, 'How is uni going?'

Lona replies, 'I dropped out of uni five asks of that question ago,' or more likely she replies with something politer and less true.

Grandpa barely utters a word. He doesn't even seem particularly interested or pleased about the fact Lona is around. This hurts Lona in a mosaic of small ways. She asks him if he enjoyed the audio book she gave him for his birthday.

'I…haven't…listened to it yet,' he says slowly. His expression is pained, and Lona wonders if he's having issues with the CD player.

After dinner, she pops her head into Ben's old room to see if the stereo is still connected, or if Mum's moved it while she was tidying up. It's still plugged in and working, but there's no sign Grandpa's even tried to use it. The case for the audio book has been slotted onto the shelf between all the other neglected books.

Deflated, Lona retreats to her bedroom. There's a big patch of not-faded carpet where the bed used to be. She doesn't know where to sit, seeing as she always used to sit on the edge of the bed and stare at herself sitting on the edge of the bed in the mirror. She sits on the desk chair, but it's not the same. The bookshelves on her walls are empty caves. She opens her desk drawer and sees all the black plastic canisters with grey plastic lids, full of undeveloped film. She shuts the drawer, then opens it again.

There's a tote bag hanging from her doorknob, featuring a faded print of Van Gogh's *Skull of a Skeleton with Burning Cigarette* on one side. She fills it with the film canisters and slings it over her shoulder. Chucks a couple more t-shirts and a discoloured soft-toy Hedwig on top of them.

She goes out and waves a hand around, announcing her departure.

When she leaves Mum, Dad, Grandpa, Ben, Harriet, she forces herself to say it like: I've got to go home. She declines a lift to the train station. She walks.

Cup weekend

Lona goes to the art department on a Monday afternoon early in November. It's the Melbourne Cup weekend, so she's hoping no one much will be around. She takes the staircase up to the second floor photo media lab. The darkroom is empty, the IN USE sign unlit.

Between her and the glorious, silent black of its walls is Tristan. He's in the printmaking classroom rolling a slab of set text through the printmaker, making flyers for a Marxist Ideas conference.

Lona wonders what he's doing here, what he's always doing here. Maybe it's the more successful, more talented wife thing. Maybe it's because he likes being alone. Maybe he's not meant to be here either.

Lona stands at the end of the hallway and she knows she's defeated. Her bag full of undeveloped film bumps against her leg. She considers turning the bathroom at the sharehouse into a darkroom. She considers Sim and Rach banging on the door saying they've got to get their hairdryer and get ready right this very minute.

There's a part of Lona that has always enjoyed giving up, that has always been slightly relieved when she does. It's so much easier than trying to make things work.

There's a squeak as she turns around. Maybe Tristan hears, maybe he looks up. It wouldn't matter. The girl is gone.

The real reason

The real reason Lona dropped out of art school was because there wasn't a reason. There was just this hollowed-out space inside of her stomach that made her feel sick and sad all the time and all she knew was that there wasn't a reason for any of it: the studying art, the not studying art, the making art, the not making art.

So: anything else. Anything other than the thing she loves, because if the thing she loves doesn't make her happy, then what's the point. Pushing shopping trolleys around can distract her if she lets it. At least she never expects it to make her whole.

Emoticons

Lona messages George. She asks him if he wants to be pretentious and boring and go see the new exhibition at the NGV. She uses the smirking face and the flexed biceps to indicate irony and self-awareness. She takes emoticons extremely seriously. She takes them so seriously that she refuses to call them emojis, because she considers *emoji* a ridiculous, unserious word. (She will at some point in her life realise that *emoji* is a Japanese word and then wonder if this makes her a white supremacist.)

George doesn't reply for four-and-a-half gruelling hours. He sends back:

Yeah sounds amazing! (WOMAN DANCING) (OK HAND) (PERSON GETTING MASSAGE) (ALIEN) (SAXOPHONE)

Lona is understandably confused, but she is pretty certain she just wrangled a date, so she is pretty certain she is happy. She replies:

Great (THUMBS UP)

NGV

They meet at Flinders Street station and walk up to the National Gallery of Victoria. Lona asks if they can just not do the small talk thing and George says, 'I think I am my mother's least favourite son.'

Lona says, 'I have an anxiety problem.'

It is Friday night, the gallery is open late. Lona has asked for time off from work specifically. Pat's husband Bill is DJ-ing the roller disco at Planet Skate tonight. The kids are in for a lot of Phil Collins and disappointment. Lona and George have to line up for tickets, which means they have to stand close and maintain consistent conversation. They talk about what other exhibitions they've previously seen here. It is not scintillating, but it is something.

The current exhibition is a collection of clay pots. The clay pots are purportedly culturally and artistically significant. Lona is known for being: an art person. She herself often makes the mistake of believing about herself what everyone else does: that she must like galleries because she is an art person. By the third room of clay pots, Lona remembers that she is not an art person so much as: a person who makes art but has no real interest in walking around a room and staring at art.

She also realises that going to a gallery is a terrible idea for a date, despite what movies and books have always suggested. George seems far more interested in the clay pots than she is. He spends more than five seconds on each, which makes no godly sense to Lona. Thus, they are moving through the exhibition at different speeds.

She sees him, occasionally, across the room. She spends half an hour in the gift shop afterwards waiting for him to spurt out of the exit. She buys a tiny clay pot for Grandpa. She makes peace with the fact she will never see George again after tonight's spectacular failure. He appears and says, 'Lost you there. That was fascinating. Do you want to get something to eat?'

'Um,' she says. 'Sure.'

Doing something nice

George takes her to a bar with glowing mushrooms on the ceiling. The cocktails are all named after books. He thinks that because she likes reading she will like a room that is full of people and has books painted on the walls. She doesn't have the heart to tell him she much prefers rooms with no people in them that have books you can actually read. He is doing something nice for her. She feels like doing something nice for him, i.e. keeping her mouth shut.

Their knuckles brush like cowards against separate ends of the tabletop. Lona uses her front teeth to peel a strip of pink-grey flesh from her bottom lip. It takes a moment for her to laugh at what George has just said. His relief when she does is a barely audible release of air.

In a film there would be: the cut to, the fingertips numbed on shirt buttons, the breath and the soft black. In this glance there is: the fear and the wanting to move, the not moving. Lona asks, 'You got much on for the weekend?'

He says, 'I'm not sure.'

The unfettered fervour with which Lona wants to climb into that weekend and make it hers is frightening. Her knees are weak at the thought of it. Her head is going warm with the whisky.

She slides her fingers into the hair at the back of her scalp. He's watching her and the thought is simultaneous, is the only thought the night was ever thinking.

Hotel Windsor

They walk to Parliament, elbows bumping. Lona stops to point out a large spider that's crawling across a window of the Hotel Windsor and when she turns around George is there, so very close, and so very not paying attention to the spider. He moves suddenly and then his mouth is on her mouth and there's the initial surprise of it: the mashing of lips together. Then there's the surprise of it being over before it properly got started.

He stares at her and she stares at him and then his hand is on that tingling skin at the back of her neck and there's the tentative way she tilts her face up towards him so that her lips find his and this time it's slower and lovelier.

Cold metal bench

They do their goodnighting in the pale, glaring light of the Parliament station bowels. Lona is relieved that there is no invitation. She is afraid of accepting out of politeness. Even more afraid of accepting out of not-politeness.

George's train is leaving in five minutes. The next one isn't for an hour. He swallows and his Adam's apple shifts. He says, 'I had a good time.'

There's another kiss, a delicate, broken-winged moth of a kiss, and then he goes. Lona has twelve minutes of sitting on a cold, metal bench until her train. She can't stop smiling.

Voicemail

In the staffroom at the back of Coles, Lona pulls her bag out of her locker. She's just come off an eight-hour trolley shift and is, as a result, dead. She tugs her phone out in case Tab or George has texted and she finds two missed calls from Mum.

She accesses voicemail and listens to the messages: Mum's at the hospital. Grandpa has pneumonia. He's all right. Thought you should know.

Lona heads straight to the train station and catches a train towards the city. She doesn't know where she's going. She calls Mum and Mum sounds stressed but not distraught. The not sounding distraught comforts Lona.

Lona tells her she's on her way. Mum says she doesn't need to come if it's too much hassle. Lona says just tell me where. Mum says ok.

Lona doesn't like using GPS on her phone. She hates that you can only see a few hundred metres ahead of you at a time and that you never end up remembering how to get home again. She likes physical maps and she likes sitting down and looking at them before she even leaves home. She likes knowing exactly where she's going and exactly how it fits in with her understanding of where things are.

She gets off at South Yarra and brings up Maps on her phone. She walks with all of everything, everywhere held in her palm and she doesn't have the time or the headspace to be annoyed.

The Alfred

Mum's still at the Alfred when Lona gets there. Lona finds hospitals intimidating and confusingly clean and unclean at the same time. She has to go up a specific lift to be able to access another specific lift that takes her to room 18 in C-wing.

Grandpa has been moved out of emergency. He is stable, but weak. Mum grabs Lona's arm the minute she arrives and pulls her up to the bed. 'Dad, look who's here!'

Grandpa looks at her through eyelids heavy with medication. 'Lona,' he says breathlessly. His voice whistles with air. Fluid on the lungs.

'How are you feeling?' she asks, and even though she knows it's a stupid question, she doesn't know what else to say and any words in her mouth feel better than none.

He grimaces. 'Not too bad. Don't you worry.'

Mum jams another pillow under his head. 'You gave us a fright, Dad. A real fright.' She's shaking, agitated. Like Lona gets when she feels things slipping out of her control.

Lona pats Mum's shoulder. 'You want to go get some coffee? I'll sit with Grandpa for a bit.'

Mum is reluctant, but she's also worn-out. She looks overtired. Maybe she hasn't been sleeping well. Lona doesn't know why. She doesn't know how to ask. Mum is wearing clothes Lona's never seen before. It's a new, strange, meaningless feeling in Lona's chest: the not being there to notice when things change.

Mum goes down to Alf's Cafe in the lobby. Lona sits on the chair beside the bed with the seat cushion that's stained in places you don't want a seat to be stained. Grandpa is struggling to keep his eyes open.

'You want me to read?' Lona asks. She gets out her book. It's a wartime romance about a smart, capable woman and an intense, guilt-ridden man. There are secondary characters called Bunty and Cecil. There are always secondary characters called Bunty and Cecil. Lona reads aloud about the Blitz, the same Blitz she knows Grandpa lived through, that he was evacuated to Wales because of. She's never asked him about that part of his life. Never asked him about any part of his life.

Mum gets back with a coffee and pulls in another chair from the hallway. Lona has stopped reading, the book open on her lap. 'Go on,' Mum says.

Second date

Lona and George go out for dinner. She keeps zoning out in the middle of telling him things, the words falling out of her head as she's saying them.

'Are you all right?' George asks.

She says, 'My grandpa's in hospital.'

'I'm sorry,' he says. 'Are you close?'

She slides her knife and fork around her empty plate. 'I don't know.' She's halfway through an Aperol spritz, but it's just making her tired. She's wearing blue mascara and green eye shadow. She's wearing a top that has a picture of Leia Organa on it with the caption: Don't call me princess. The word *princess* is hidden where the t-shirt is tucked into her skirt, so it just says: Don't call me. Lona has always liked that.

The second date is worse than the first because most of the easy stuff has already been said. The restaurant is loud and dimly lit. Lona feels like she's in an underexposed photograph. She feels blurry at the edges and suffocated by her inability to see and hear properly. The night is dreamlike. It's hard for her to care about how she's coming across when none of it seems real.

It's late November warm outside. George won't stop looking at her like he's trying to work her out. She can't stop avoiding his eye.

There's an ice cream shop a couple of doors down. They go inside as if they've somehow made the decision to do so without any words being exchanged. There are three freezer cabinets filled with every possible flavour: tiramisu, green tea, watermelon and feta, baklava, black pepper.

'What would you like?' George asks.

'Chocolate,' Lona says.

'Double chocolate? White chocolate? Chocolate chip?' he suggests. 'There's a mocha. Oh, and a chocolate caramel swirl.'

'Just plain chocolate,' she says.

'You can have two scoops? Two different flavours?'

'Two scoops of chocolate is fine. Or one scoop. Whatever.'

George gives her a weird look. They eat out the front on plastic chairs. George cannot let it go. 'Plain chocolate?' he insists. 'What's the point in getting plain chocolate when there are so many other flavours you can't get at the supermarket?'

She shrugs. 'What's the point in not getting plain chocolate when you know that plain chocolate is the greatest of all flavours?'

'How do you know that plain chocolate is the greatest of all flavours if you haven't tried all flavours?'

'Blessed ignorance.'

It may be the sweet potato ice cream that he's eating that is making George look so concerned, but Lona has a feeling it's her.

'I feel like I should be one hundred per cent honest with you before this goes any further,' she says. 'I like chocolate ice cream. I like plain chips. I like toast with butter on it. Just butter, nothing else. I like Hugh Grant movies. I get mild sauce on my chicken at Nando's. I drink vodka with cranberry juice. I'm bland. I enjoy my blandness. I delight in doing the same things over and over again.'

George shakes his head. 'I had you completely wrong.'

'Everyone does. Don't let the air of arty pretentiousness deceive you. I'm actually the most basic bitch alive.'

George leans over and kisses her, both of their lips cold and numb. 'I like you Lona Wallace,' he says, as if it's that easy.

Different room

Lona meets Ben at his office after work and he drives them to the Alfred to visit Grandpa. It's just the two of them, so they spend the car ride swapping *Community* references and comments about the music that's playing. Lona used to listen to whatever Ben listened to and it drove him mad. More than that, it drove him to metal, a place he knew even Lona wouldn't follow. His car stereo doesn't have bluetooth or an AUX plug, but it does have a five-stack CD player and a glove box full of mix CDs compiled by an angsty, pre-metal Ben. Lona blasts Evanescence all the way to the hospital.

Grandpa's been moved to a different room. It has three other people in it. They are separated only by curtains. After several weeks of sleeping in the living room behind a sheet, Lona understands this discomfort.

Grandpa is watching a quiz show on the TV when they arrive. The sound isn't on, he can't hear any of the questions or answers or read the subtitles. This momentarily stakes Lona through the heart. He's sitting up at least. Ben offers him the muffin they brought downstairs. Grandpa can't stomach it. He pulls a face.

Lona and Ben shoulder the conversational weight, propping it up for their uninterested third party. Grandpa is tetchy and tired. He doesn't want to be there but it feels like: he doesn't want them to be there.

In the lift when they leave, Ben says, 'Maybe it'd be different if we'd spent more time with him when we were growing up. Actually got to know him, you know.'

Lona uses the antibacterial gel pump in the lobby. She wants to sterilise herself of this place, this hurt.

A series of messages

George messages: what are you doing atm? Like he expects the answer to ever be anything other than: skimming *Half-Blood Prince* for the hefty doses of adolescent angst in an effort to momentarily escape the tedium of existence.

She tells him what she's reading. First as a joke, and then because he genuinely seems interested. She tells him:

Reading Ulysses (FLEXED BICEPS)

He says things like:

Impressive

She says things like:

Would you be equally impressed if I admitted I am

actually reading a book about teenage wizards?

He types like a lightning strike, speech bubble after speech bubble cracking into existence:

I love teenage wizard books

Also books where teenagers go on dates and have friends

All things I never experienced as an actual teenager

What happens is: she's smitten.

All the details

Tab wants all the details. She says that she is experiencing whiplash. 'I thought you weren't into him! Now I hear from Nick you've seen each other—TWICE!' The level of enthusiasm Tab is showing for the knowledge that Lona has twice been in the romantic company of a man is mildly insulting.

Lona shrugs like it's no biggie. 'Yeah, well.'

'Sooooo...' Tab says eagerly.

Lona experiences the stomach-juice-curdling feeling that accompanies being asked to dredge up what he said and what she said and dissect it in the company of others. Lona does enough of that on her own time. She does not need a public forum for discussion.

'I...like him,' she says, somewhat uncertainly.

'Yeah?' Tab encourages.

'We've...made out a couple of times,' she murmurs, somewhat embarrassedly.

'Yeah?'

'Well, what do you want to know?' she demands, somewhat defensively.

Tab sighs a big, loud sigh. 'What do you want to tell me?' she asks.

Lona considers her options. 'I would like to leave it at that,' she says.

Tab is both disappointed and amused. She rolls her eyes and laughs. They are at a cafe in Oakleigh eating garlic-soaked souvlakis. Lona has pulled out her tomatoes and swapped them for Tab's onions. It's been ages since Lona has seen Tab one-on-one without Nick. She can't help feeling panicked about it ending before she's even started to enjoy it. It's making her weird and conversationally uncooperative.

'I want to do something fun,' Tab says. 'Something spontaneous.'

'There's a cool historical graveyard up the road,' Lona says.

'Something spontaneous and not creepy,' Tab clarifies.

They go into the city to play mini golf at Holey Moley. They order a sharing cocktail that's an ambiguous mix of vodka, Red Bull, whisky and lemonade, and is served in a large trophy cup. They get daytime drunk and putt around the course. Lona tries to keep track of the score because she's the kind of person who's overly competitive when she's pretty sure she's winning. Tab juggles any golf balls she can get her hands on. Someone complains. They are removed from the facility.

They come home via the graveyard where they sit with their backs against a lichen-covered headstone and Tab says, 'This graveyard is beautiful. I want to die here.'

Lona says, 'That's not how graveyards work.'

It's dusk and the lampposts are lit up along all the paths and they're orange orbs floating against the dark denim-blue sky. Tab fits her head into the Tab-shaped crook of Lona's neck and they tell each other things they've told each other a hundred times before. 'I like him,' Lona says.

This time Tab just nods.

Drive-in

Nick drives them out to the Lunar Drive-in. It's a sticky summer night and Tab's flashing her hairy pits in a sleeveless summer dress as she reaches up to open the boot. They've brought folding chairs along with them. Tab's picnic rug, too: for if anyone's feeling particularly frisky. Nick tunes the car radio to the Drive-in frequency and keeps the keys in the ignition and the windows open.

'Suckers,' Tab remarks, looking at the people still crammed inside their cars. '*This* is how you drive-in.'

Lona and Tab have brought chips and chocolate and sour snakes. Nick has brought beetroot chips and a tub of hummus.

'Honey, I don't think we can see each other anymore,' Tab says.

George offers to get some popcorn from the diner.

Lona goes with him. She likes the way it feels to walk with him and wait in line with him and be seen with him. She likes the way he doesn't try to hold her hand, but he does walk close enough that their arms keep brushing.

The movie is about a bunch of people trapped inside a spaceship with an alien life form that gets more powerful every time it kills. This is Lona's favourite genre of movie even though she hates the gory bits. She likes having George there because she can say things like: can I open my eyes now.

He probably thinks it's cute and feminine, whereas she thinks it's the logical and natural response to seeing Ryan Reynolds get eaten from the inside out.

Tab and Nick are sprawled on the picnic rug, with their shoes kicked aside and their arms folded under their heads. They kiss occasionally in the boring, sciencey bits. Light, little kisses that send a light, little thrill through Lona's stomach that is half nausea and half a want for George to kiss her like that.

George is watching the film intently. A mosquito lands on Lona's arm and she slaps at it and ends up with someone else's blood on her skin. Nick has brought hand sanitiser because of course Nick has thought to bring hand sanitiser.

George says, 'I've never been bitten by a mosquito.'

Lona says, 'I don't believe you.'

His phone rings and he looks at the screen and it's his mum calling and he groans. The movie's almost at the end, but he takes it anyway. She can hear him talking fast in Mandarin around the other side of the car. She claps a hand over her eyes because the alien is doing some super creepy shit she doesn't want to see.

'You can open them now,' George says, and he's back again.

She smiles at him. 'What was that about?'

'Ah, nothing.' The movie's still going, but he's looking at her now. Their chairs are tight together, back legs sinking into the grass. She's feeling kind of sweaty and gross from the heat and the nerves. His pinky finger finds hers on the plastic armrest and she guesses that there's at least a seventy-five per cent chance he's going to kiss her. She realises she's never calculated the possibility of her making the first move and this feels like a massive oversight.

She doesn't have to lean in very far before George is there, meeting her at something close to halfway. The kiss is slow, bruising. Tab throws a sandal at them. It's one of the European comfort shoe brand sandals that Tab calls her Grandad Shoes. 'Get a room,' she calls gleefully.

Lona's head is a blood rush. Her lips feel tender. She misses the feel of George's mouth on them already. The credits are rolling.

In the car on the way home he talks about how his younger brother is always waking him up by practising his scales on the piano at 5 a.m. He talks about how his mother refuses to let any of them eat dinner unless they're all at the table together, which he finds infuriating and nice at the same time. It takes a while in Lona's lust drunk mind, but she realises dully that he's making it clear to her: he's not going to invite her back because he still lives at home.

And so, it seems, the proverbial ball is in Lona's proverbial court. She does not know what to do with the proverbial ball, so she just rolls it aside for the moment.

'I've got to get up insanely early tomorrow,' she announces to the car at large. This is only true if a person considers 9.30 a.m. insanely early. She looks across at George in the back seat and there's a bit of her that wants to just do it. Get it over with. Retract her previous statement and make a simple offer like: coffee, or a beverage of the more alcoholic variety.

'That sucks,' he says.

She sits on her hands both literally and figuratively. Nick drops her out the front of her place and George gets out just to walk her to the door. 'Goodnight,' she says. It ends with the closing of the door on all other possibilities than: both of them alone, wishing that they weren't.

Christmas at the hospital

This year the Wallaces do two Christmases. One at home and one at the hospital with Grandpa. He's gotten over the pneumonia, but he picked up a staph infection in the process. Mum's furious about it, won't stop going on about how hospitals are a hotbed for disease and infection. Dad is unsuccessful in pointing out they are also a hotbed for making people better.

Grandpa is not complaining. He is barely even speaking. Christmas at the hospital is bleakly Dickensian. The nurses bring around trays of cold turkey and congealed gravy, which are expressionlessly consumed by patients whose families have not showed up with something better.

Lona unwraps Grandpa's presents for him. White y-fronts and a pair of slippers. Lona chipped in some dosh for the undies. She was too dispirited by the audio book's reception to go the extra mile this time. They eat fruitcake and drink champagne. Mum brought enough glasses for the other patients in the room. There is a radio playing Bing Crosby. It is rendered completely inaudible every few minutes by the sound of a patient moaning or an alarm going screech screech screech.

Festivities are interrupted for blood pressure tests and the emptying of catheter bags. 'I've got to get out of here,' Grandpa says more than once. He legs are so lacking in muscle he can't lift them by himself. He gets Dad and Ben to roll him onto his side.

'What's going to happen?' Lona asks in the car on the way home.

'We're going to have dinner, then we'll do presents,' Mum says. She knows that's not what Lona's asking about.

Back at the house they have the full meal. Aunty Jas and Uncle Phil and Cousin Rob and Cousin Ed arrive bearing a bowl of coleslaw and a box of Cadbury Favourites.

Mum's hair is curling around her face from the sweat and grease of sticking her face in the oven. Dad takes over gin and tonic duty, slicing lemon as he trills along to a boppy early-noughties cover of 'The Little Boy That Santa Claus Forgot'. The potatoes are phenomenal, like always. The turkey is not as good as chicken, like always. They pull Christmas crackers and everyone wears the paper hats that slip over their eyes except for Ed, who's seventeen and has combed his hair back in a very particular, apparently delicate, way.

Gifts are exchanged over pudding drenched in white sauce. Lona gets a stack of film for her Polaroid camera and a bookshelf that Mum wrapped by simply throwing an entire roll of paper over the top of it. 'Tab said your place is a mess,' she tells Lona, her voice stinging slightly because Lona still hasn't invited her parents around to see her new home.

'Do you want to help me drive the bookshelf over there tomorrow?' Lona asks, bluntly snapping off the olive branch.

Mum shrugs indifferently. 'I guess I could.'

Lona smiles, and so does Mum, but only when the other's not looking.

Later, Lona calls George. He doesn't do Christmas, but he wishes her a good one all the same. 'It sounds chaotic over there,' he remarks. She explains that they've just started their annual game of charades.

'I need to meet your family,' he says, and he's being

about 59 per cent serious. They talk a while and neither of her parents tell her to: get off the phone and spend time with your family. This is most likely because they are relieved that Lona has finally got herself a boyfriend. Lona is less incensed by this injustice than she would've been before said boyfriend inserted himself in her life.

Lona tells George about the potatoes and the bookshelf. She tells him about Grandpa's legs and Cousin Ed's gravity-defying hair. George asks her questions like these things actually hold any interest for him. It's bewildering to Lona. She doesn't know what's going on. She forgets to ask questions of her own, which leads her to the conclusion: she's a bad girlfriend and/or human being in general.

She hangs up at the end of their see you tomorrowing, and she's confused and pleased and exhausted. She is not sure that she can sustain this thing, this feeling of bewildered happiness. It relies so much on someone else and Lona has never relied so much on someone else. It is terrifying.

The Jam Factory

Lona and George meet at the Jam Factory. He wants to see a Spanish film that he says has been generating festival buzz. She just wants to see him. They get to the front of the queue and the boy behind the desk tells them the screening of *The Passion of Wild Doves* has been cancelled. He asks if they want to see another film instead.

The options are:

a) disgruntled man saves wife and world
b) disgruntled man saves world and wife
c) a young, yet-to-be-disgruntled man gets a wife and saves the world
d) special anniversary screening of *What Women Want*

'The Vin Diesel one, it is,' Lona says. She pulls out her wallet. It's small enough to fit in the pocket of her jeans. Lona is bewildered by women's wallets: big, fat steaks of leather jammed with a hundred loyalty cards, spilling faded EFTPOS receipts. She has six cards in her wallet: bank, ID, library, MYKI, expired student concession and flybuys. The wallet has pictures of cats on it. Cat butts, to be specific. A cat butt field guide, to be even more specific. American short hair, Siamese, black and white, Siberian, Persian.

George takes the wallet from her and says, 'That's weird.'

Lona had exactly the same reaction when Tab gave her the wallet two Christmases ago, but she is deeply offended nonetheless. She snatches it back. The wallet is made of plastic. It has begun to deteriorate, mainly from being jammed in her back pocket and sat on.

She pulls out a twenty, but George holds a hand over her own. 'Nah, I've got this.'

He fishes out his wallet. Classic man wallet. Dark brown leather that folds over itself. A tiny coin pouch in the centre. Thankfully no blatant condom ring.

'It's all good,' Lona says, shoving the bank note at the boy behind the counter.

'Put it on card,' George insists, ignoring her.

The boy looks between them and she can tell he's about to take George's card because: the man should pay. But Lona slams the twenty down on his keyboard. 'Take the goddamn money,' she says.

Cinema 12

Lona lets George pay for the popcorn so he can recover his masculinity. In cinema 12, they stumble hands out through the dark to find their seats. A couple of pimpled youths are sitting in them. Lona and George do the thing where they look obviously at their tickets and then around for their seats, but the youths don't even glance at them. They have their hoods cinched tight around their faces and their Nikes kicked up on the seats in front of them. They're not going anywhere.

Neither Lona nor George says anything. They take the next seats along. They will stew in their resentment in silence, as is their god-given right.

The ads start. There's a ratio of about one movie trailer for every reminder to switch off your phone. Lona can hear herself chewing her popcorn and she wonders if George can too. The youths are on their phones. Every few minutes one erupts with the unintelligible cacophony of a snapchat story. Lona is giving them her fiercest side eye, attempting to convey something along the lines of: will you please shut up, can't you see some of us are trying to enjoy this ad for TGI Friday's. George leans over her and says, 'Hey, you mind?'

Lona goes rigid like a dead animal. Her wildest dream and most hideous nightmare has come true. Her gentleman caller has: done something about it.

The youths respond with the timeless classic: 'Oi, fuck off.'

Someone down the front yells out, 'Shut up back there!'

'Come up here and make me!' one of the youths hollers.

The movie is starting. The man down the front has thrown a middle finger back at the youths and now they're jostling in their seats. Lona looks at George. 'How much do you want to see Vin Diesel's pecs protect the universe?'

On the escalators on the way out George stands backwards and even though she's on the step above him, they're staring straight into each other's faces. He says, 'I don't know why, but I'm getting a hankering for TGI Friday's.'

Hello Hello

George's band plays at the Curtin. They are an eight-piece ensemble called Hello Hello, after the Cat Empire. Tab gets a margarita and Nick gets a whisky sour, the same as Lona, much to her dismay.

There are a lot of people who know George, who like George, who squeeze his shoulders and give him a good ribbing between sets. Lona feels swamped by it, made redundant by it. There's another feeling though, a gut-deep feeling, something like pride. Seeing him up there, hand around the neck of the bass, rocking in time. He is hers to hold, to press her lips to after and say, 'Shit, you're hot.'

She is the one he wants, out of this room, out of this world. She's the one he wants touching him. She's mellow spirit drunk. George is glassy beer drunk. They Uber back to hers touching touching touching but when they get there she says: it shouldn't be like this. Not the first time.

It's been weeks now, since the NGV, since the first time she recognised the acute possibility of this eventuality. Lona has explained it to him: the virgin thing. She has also explained to him: the anxiety thing.

He has nodded and assured her that it's no big deal. But what he is missing is that it is a big deal. It is Lona's deal. These are parts of Lona that she has learnt how to circumnavigate. She does not like it when the map changes. She does not like it when she can only see a few hundred metres ahead.

This time, after the Curtin, she can tell that George is pissed. He doesn't say anything other than, 'All right,' but it's obvious. She's pissed too, at herself and at him. They're breathing hard in each other's faces and she can still feel the blood hot where he was just beginning to touch her. She can feel him hard against her leg.

He gets up for water and maybe to get away from her.

Pulls back the sheet curtain and steps through. She doesn't know what she wants it to be like or what it will take. She's not entirely sure what's stopping her at this point beyond: she's been so long like this.

He comes back and the anger's gone. He lies down beside her and brushes the hair away from her face, kisses her on the spot just above her left eyebrow. She wants very badly to take his hands and put them on those aching places.

She says, 'You want to watch *Game of Thrones*?'

Second stall from the left

Lona leaves 5 Seconds of Summer playing while she goes to the toilet. Planet Skate is swarming and all the way to the bathroom she has kids yelling requests at her from inside the rink.

'I'm not playing Kendrick Lamar,' she says for the millionth time. 'Do you want me to lose my job?'

'Yes!' a mulleted young chap yells back.

She bumps the sides of her fists together like Ross does to Monica in *Friends*, and they are all too young to understand or be offended by the reference.

The bathroom is full of giggling girls when she pushes open the door. There are two or three by the mirror swapping Lip Smackers. They are still in their skates and are finding it difficult to stand up straight on the slippery floor surface. A tall girl comes out of one of the stalls with too much speed and smacks into the sink.

'Ouch,' she says, gripping her stomach.

All of them glance at Lona with a mixture of interest and ambivalence. She locks herself in her favourite stall (second from the left) and sits down for a blissful couple of minutes of not having to look at or be looked at by anyone.

The girls leave and so does their chatter. All that's left is the dulled sensation of fourth- or fifth- or whatever-wave pop punk making Planet Skate's foundations groan.

The door to the bathroom croaks open and a couple more sets of wheels glide in. 'Look at this,' one of the girls says.

'Oh my god, you look amazing!'

'Here hold my phone a second while I get...' There is the sound of a bottle being unscrewed. 'Try this.'

A second later: 'Ugh, what's in this?'

'It's Dad's. Like, sambucha or something.'

'It tastes like liquorice.'

Lona flushes the toilet and closes the lid like a good girl. When she opens the door of the stall and steps out, arms crossed, the girls are facing the mirror, fixing their hair. They look young enough to still be playing with Bratz dolls. They watch Lona out of the corner of their eyes as she steps up to the sink and washes her hands. Without speaking, they both turn to leave.

'Hold up,' Lona says, holding out a hand.

She half-expects them not to stop. She doesn't even know what she's doing, what she's going to do. 'Give it to me,' she says, flexing her fingers in a gimme gimme gimme a man after midnight motion.

The girls look at her blankly. 'What?'

'Give me the flask,' she says, guessing.

They share a glance. If they were twelve-year-old Lonas they would have already handed it over. Not that a twelve-year-old Lona would have ever thought it was a good idea, or even a particularly worthy cause, to sneak alcohol into Planet Skate. The thought wouldn't have even crossed her mind. These girls aren't like Lona, and she can see they're about *this* close to rolling their eyes and pushing their way out of the bathroom. They probably know that Lona wouldn't go to any great lengths to stop them. They probably know they intimidate her with their ne'er-do-well behaviour that shamefully reminds Lona that she has never even dabbled in ne'er-do-well behaviour. But they don't move. The girl on the left has three studs in her earlobe, which seems insane for a twelve-year-old. But she's also wearing a t-shirt with a picture of iCarly on it.

She huffs and pulls a small plastic bottle out of her jacket pocket. There is a colourless liquid sloshing around inside of it. Lona takes it and the girls stand there like they are waiting to be chided. Lona had forgotten that part was necessary. She says, 'Didn't Harold the Giraffe tell you that alcohol kills brain cells?'

iCarly says, 'What's Harold the Giraffe?'

'From the Life Education van,' Lona says incredulously, to an absolute lack of reaction. 'It comes to your school?

A woman sticks her hand up Harold's sock-puppet butt and he tells you not to smoke? Geez, how the hell are you meant to be educated about life?'

She can tell she is freaking out the children. The sock-puppet butt thing probably did it. 'Ah, get out of here,' she says, waving a hand at them.

They oblige eagerly, muttering loudly as they scoot out. Lona stares at the bottle of sambuca in her right hand. Feels the thick soup of satisfaction and self-loathing that comes from being a lifelong goody-two-shoes.

She hesitates, but of course she tips it down the sink. She makes sure she rinses the bottle out properly before putting it in the recycle bin.

IKEA

Lona decides to make the dreaded pilgrimage to IKEA. The one-kilometre-long store in Springvale. She brings Tab with her, and Tab brings Nick with her, and Nick brings his little sister with him. Nick's sister's name is Cassidy. She is fourteen and loves IKEA. She loves IKEA with the kind of enthusiasm that a child is only able to muster before the world has broken them.

Lona has forgotten how infuriating IKEA is. She has fond memories of it because Mum used to dump her in the ball pit before heading inside. Outside of the ball pit, IKEA operates like the ten circles of hell. Just when she thinks they've reached the end, she realises they're only up to the kitchen display section. It is detrimental to stray from the marked path because this only leads to becoming stranded in the warehouse.

IKEA makes her resent her parents for never buying her an elevated bed with a built-in alcove study desk. IKEA makes her resent herself for living in a house that has a plastic crate instead of a television stand. IKEA compels her to buy useless crap just so she feels justified in having spent three hours attempting to navigate the shortcuts and having infuriatingly ended up back where they started.

Cassidy is enthralled. Nick says, 'I apologise for my psycho little sis,' but in this really loving older brother way that Lona can see makes Tab's ovaries ache, whether Tab wants them to or not. Tab and Nick peruse stacks of decorative hourglasses with some part of their bodies always attached. They buy wine tumblers and ice trays with moulds shaped like little boats. Cassidy jumps on every bed they pass.

Lona eventually finds what she came for: a folding room divider. It's plastic made to look like wood which is made to look like it has cherry blossoms on it. It is kitsch beyond belief. It is most likely culturally inappropriate. Lona says, 'This is the one.'

New thingo

'You've got a new thingo,' George says, nodding at the room divider. Lona wipes her eyes with the back of her hand and nods. Her eyes are blurry with tears. She is dicing onions. 'You need some help there?' he asks.

'No, no, all good,' she says, brushing the onions into the saucepan. Her eyes continue to stream. She can't help taking this as a bad sign.

She's nervous. George doesn't know why, because George doesn't know that a decision has been made. George doesn't know that the new thingo is a symbol, that it is a metaphorical, as well as literal, structure.

The sheet pegged to a piece of string is gone. Her single bed and her books, now neatly stacked in a bookshelf, are completely out of view. The room divider is tacky and wonderful. Lona is making minestrone soup.

Sim and Rach careen in and out of the living room looking for their phones and their keys and their lip-gloss. They are getting ready. They have been getting ready since four in the afternoon. Sim is curling her straight hair and Rach is straightening her curly hair. Faces are done and outfits are swapped twice.

'Lona, can I borrow your denim jacket?' Sim asks. Lona says ok, yes, but it's Rach who ends up wearing it over her printed jumpsuit.

The soup's just started to boil by the time they finally leave for their party. 'You guys should totally come,' Sim offers half-heartedly, knowing there's no way she's dragging Lona off the couch on a Saturday night.

'Another time,' Lona says.

George has the news on. It's just them, alone in the house, and she's cooking soup and he's watching the seven o'clock news. George asks, 'What's so funny?' because she's bent over laughing.

They eat on the couch and watch the last ten minutes of *Spider Man 3* on Channel 7 and then the last ten minutes of *The Incredible Hulk* on Go!. Lona's bowl is a fifty/fifty split of soup and parmesan cheese. George brings up Netflix and starts the mind- and soul-destroying process that is: deciding what to watch. Lona puts down her empty bowl and takes the remote from him. He says, 'I swear, if you make me watch *The Social Network* one more time...'

She shuts him up in the most efficient way possible, covering his mouth with her own. '*The Social Network* is a seminal modern classic,' she says, and then she kisses him again, harder and more insistent.

There is a point in the running of a tongue around inside another person's mouth that it goes from being the main act to the support artist. There is the being horizontal with her on him and the little moan he makes when she presses her lips to the base of his jaw. There is the hot feeling between her legs and the pressure at the front of his jeans.

She slides a hand down and she finds him, finds a way to make his breath catch. She is surprised by how powerful she is, how powerless. The difference just a matter of him touching her touching him touching. His fingers slip inside her underwear and she freezes momentarily, pulls away from him and the screaming famine of it.

He exhales, mistakes her, whispers, 'Are you sure you

want to do this?' But this is not a question Lona wants to be asked. She wants to be reckless with her surety.

'Yes,' she says.

In the after

There is hurt in it, and an almost excruciating closeness. In the after there is bleeding and holding. His thumb brushes over her forehead. 'How do you feel?' he asks.

This is too enormous a question. She kisses his bottom lip and leans her head against his chest.

'Overwhelmingly,' she whispers, the word just breath on his skin.

West Footscray

George walks Lona back to West Footscray station. She is squeezing her hands into fists and freaking out. 'Oh, Jesus, I called your mother Mrs Qiu. I've never called anyone Mrs Anything in my entire life.'

'What about at school?' George points out reasonably.

Lona is not capable of processing reason at this point in time. Lona has just met George's parents for the first time and it did not go well.

'You were fine,' George says. They bump shoulders and arms as they walk. It's almost nine. George didn't want her walking to the station on her own.

'They think I'm a deadbeat,' she whines.

'You are a deadbeat,' George reminds her. He stops her so he can kiss the side of her face and she feels prickly all over, an echidna rolling into a ball. She shrugs him off and keeps going.

'I'm going to go back to uni eventually,' she says.

George takes her hand. 'You know I'm joking.'

Her hand is hot and twitchy in his. 'Me too.'

Lona hasn't been to George's side of town before. She doesn't cross the West Gate much because there's no real point. Up until now she's always thought there was nothing over that way except Sovereign Hill and probably Adelaide eventually. She rarely leaves the south east because there's rarely a reason to.

They get to the station but the train doesn't arrive for twenty-three minutes. George sits with her. 'You look so much like your brother,' she tells him.

'I hate when people say that.'

'Why?'

The wind has picked up and it's cool. The skin of George's bare arms is beginning to goosebump. Lona asks him, 'You want my jacket?'

He gives her a look like he does when she says things that have no place in her mouth. He says, 'Nah, all good.' It's unfair because she wants to feel cold and feel good and strong about that while the one she cares about is warm. It's unfair she's not allowed.

Her train pulls in and they kiss quickly, perfunctorily. He waves from the platform like they're wartime sweethearts. It's dark by the time she gets back into the city. She runs for the Westall train with her finger jammed inside her book.

Recital

George has a recital on Wednesday night. Lona and Tab sit right up the back of the recital hall, a crisp cardboard programme unfolded on each of their laps. They have made it through Brass Section and Soprano Soloist and the Piano Wunderkind. Lona is counting them off. Five more until George's performance. Eight more until the concert ends.

She is wearing a nice dress. Black corduroy with pink roses all over it. It is, admittedly, more of a pinafore than a dress. She is, admittedly, wearing a t-shirt with Nicolas Cage's 'Not The Bees!' face on it underneath. Perhaps not exactly the definition of smart casual. Tab has her hair swept up in a patterned scarf for the occasion. She is nodding slowly with her eyes half-closed as if to express how deeply she is engaging with the music.

George appears on stage hefting his cello. It's just him and an accompanist on the grand piano. There's this big swell of silence before it starts and Lona feels an unexpected pinch in her gut. She wants this to go well for him, almost like it's her up there.

There's the first slice of a note. A few moments later there is another. His bow screeches across the strings. Then just as suddenly he is riffing back and forth, building up a storm of sound. The audience is taken aback. They look down at their programmes and confirm that what they are hearing is correct. 'Back in Black' composed by B. Johnson, A. Young and M. Young. Lona can't tell from this far back, but she doesn't think that George is smiling. He is concentrating hard, and this is music, the same as the Bach and the Handel.

Tab elbows Lona. 'He's incredible, Lone.'

She feels that swirling, giddy pride again. The crowd is murmuring. They like it, even if they won't let themselves. George strikes the strings so violently Lona is convinced one will snap. It builds up and up as the song reaches its crescendo. Each squeal grips Lona's insides. Because he's so good. He's just so, so good.

The foyer

They wait around the foyer afterwards. George's parents spot Lona and they come over.

'George was very good tonight,' Mrs Qiu says.

'Yes, very good,' Lona echoes.

Mr Qiu shakes his head. 'I don't know why he plays that shouting music.' He can't stop himself from beaming though. 'He is a stubborn boy.'

'He is,' Lona says.

The Qius look at the bunch of flowers Lona has in her hands. Pink, yellow and orange ranunculus, sagging and bruised from being kicked under her seat. 'For George,' she says, her voice coming out strangled.

'Speak of the devil,' Tab says, and there the devil is, looking glorious in a white shirt and a thin black tie. He grins bashfully at all of them as he approaches.

His mother hugs him around the waist. He's about two

feet taller than her. He looks embarrassed and pleased and his eyes catch Lona's over his mother's head. She smiles, suddenly so shy it's like this is the first time they've met. She holds the flowers out like a baton in front of her, arm straight and static. 'Good show,' she says.

He takes them, looks at them like a man will look at flowers, like: what do I do with these? Gives them a sniff even though they only smell like chemicals. 'Thanks,' he says.

George's parents want to take him out for dinner and they invite the girls along. 'It's ok,' Lona says. 'We were just going to head home.'

This is the wrong thing to say and George looks hurt. He wants her to want to hang out with his parents, but she doesn't want to hang out with anyone. George and Tab being the exceptions, and even then, not together. Tab gives her a slight nudge with her elbow. Tab is chummy with Nick's parents. She calls them Roz and Trent and they call her Sweetpea. They call everyone Sweetpea according to Nick, and according to Nick it is horrendously mortifying.

The Qius share a bemused glance. Lona grimaces at everyone's shoes. Tab says the it was lovely meeting yous and the hope you have a good evenings. She does such a good job, the Qius end up apologising to her for their not being able to make dinner. The conventions of polite discourse are restored.

George kisses Lona's cheek, keeping it G-rated for the parents. Tab gets a cheek kiss too so Lona feels like she's part of a harem. She holds the flowers for George while he goes and gets his cello. He forgets them when he leaves and she is left standing with them clutched in her hand.

Tab hooks an arm through her elbow. 'Lone, you know you should've—'

'I know,' Lona says.

Tab squeezes her wrist. 'Let's get some Macca's, hey?'

Birthday drinks

Tab organises birthday drinks for Lona. She invites all their mutual friends, possibly assuming Lona's friendship circle does not extend beyond hers. This is not unfair. It is debatable whether Lona's friendship circle extends beyond Tab herself.

Lona allows herself to be dragged out. She knows what's going on. She enjoys the charade of feigning irritation. She enjoys the effort to get her out that indicates: someone cares.

George and Nick are there when they get to the bar. Nick and Tab busy themselves with the first round. George kisses her, tasting like rum and cola, and presses a box into her hand. It's a jewellery case. There's a small drop in her belly, an: I thought you knew me better than that.

'Open it,' he says.

She does and there's a small card inside. In fast-scrawled handwriting it says: you could at least TRY to look pleased.

She looks up at him, bewildered. He says, 'Please don't

ever play poker,' and he reaches for the table behind him and hands her a parcel. She knows before she opens it that it's the collector's edition of *Six of Crows*. She's picked it up in bookshops so many times she knows its exact dimensions and the *feel* of it in her hands.

'You...'

'Are the best, I know,' he grins.

'It's not that I don't like jewellery...' she starts.

'It's just you only like it when it's something your mother has dug out of her things from the '80s, or when Tab gives you a set of hairclips shaped like cupcakes which are ridiculous but not wearing them would be even more ridiculous.' He shrugs. 'I know.'

She stares at him. She's never *said* those things. But he knows. He's noticed.

'George,' she says.

'Lona,' he says.

Nick comes over with a handful of tequila shots. Tab brings the lemon wedges and the salt. 'Happy birthday to our favourite loner,' Nick says. They chink their glasses and then lick the salt, drink the petrol and bite down on the lemon. Lona hasn't eaten since lunch. The forecast is: a somewhat messy night.

Around 9.30 p.m.

People from school and uni and nowhere in particular show up. They stand around booths until the people in them leave. Lona is pink-cheeked and loquacious. She says things that make people laugh.

Sampson arrives around 9.30 p.m. He buys Lona a pot of cider and wishes her a happy birthday. 'No longer a teenage dirtbag,' she says wistfully.

'Now just a regular dirtbag,' he comforts her.

He has done something different with his hair. It's longer and scruffier. Throw a grey hoodie on him and he'd look like the socially inept founder of a successful social media platform.

They sit out in the beer garden and talk about television shows. Sampson makes her laugh when he's being serious. There's still a part of her that wants to kiss him and touch him the way she touches George, make him shiver the way she makes George shiver. She's never been in a relationship before so she doesn't know if this is normal. She's spent all her life wanting whoever was near enough to want, and here Sampson is, leg pressed against hers on the bench seat.

Every time she leans back or forward, he does too, like he's mirroring her.

'Lona,' he says. 'I've...'

George sits down opposite with Nick. Lona makes the appropriate introductions: nerd from uni meet boyfriend and boyfriend of friend.

'Or just friend,' Nick smiles, extending a hand for Sampson to shake.

The men talk about the things men always talk about:

a) *The Simpsons*

b) men throwing and kicking around balls

c) what beer they are drinking

Tab slides in beside Lona and says, 'Thought you could escape your own party, did you?' Tab never got the memo about invading people's personal space. She is always just this side of: go away please. She rests an elbow on Lona's shoulder and assures her that her twenties are going to be the best years of her life if single-camera sitcoms set in Manhattan are anything to go by.

Sampson no longer has his leg pressed against Lona's and she misses it. George is eyeing her across the table. She asks, 'What time is it?'

'Too early to leave,' Tab says, reading her mind.

They stay out until one-something in the morning. They dance to butchered mash-ups of songs they used to like. George pogoes up and down until Lona grabs his flailing arms and puts them around her waist so that they can sway together to music that's too fast for swaying but it doesn't matter because she's never felt as good, as wanted, as his hands on that strip of hot, bare midriff can make her feel. They make out a bit like they're kids who've just met at a nightclub. Lona says, 'Take me home.'

She nearly falls asleep in the taxi. Tab is in the front seat and she's conned the driver into letting her use his AUX cord. Nick begs for anything other than Fleetwood Mac. Their Sri Lankan driver knows all the words to 'Rhiannon'. George sings and he's got this muddy amethyst of a voice and when he gets Lona into bed and pulls off her shoes and lies down and holds her, she tells him: I wish they'd played The Greatest Band Humanly Possible.

She means: I am so in love with you.

Running with the bulls

Pat and Bill have the Wallaces around for a barbeque lunch. Shrimps are not thrown on the barbie, but sausages and rissoles are. Bill cooks them until they're crusted black and indistinguishable from one another.

Jodie has been accepted for a study abroad program in Nice. She models the jacket and the jeans she's bought to take with her, the same way she and Lona used to when they'd get new polar fleece jumpers for school camp. Mum and Dad have a lot of questions for Jodie about what she's doing and where she's going. She tells them that she's planning on doing a Masters in Marie Antoinette Letting Them Eat Cake once she finishes her degree and they are impressed. Lona reserves her enthusiasm for the skerrick of edible meat she manages to extract from the centre of her rissole.

No one asks what Lona is doing or planning on doing because it is widely accepted she is having some sort of prolonged mental lapse, and it is deemed impolite to bring it up in company. She is partly relieved about this, and partly peeved.

Jodie explains that she will be staying on in Europe for an extra couple of weeks after the program ends. She has booked herself onto a fifteen-countries-in-five-drunk-days bus tour. 'I just want to see more of the world,' she says.

Lona understands that this is how she is meant to feel as a young person, but if anything, she wants to see less of the world. She wants to stay exactly where she is, stagnant, stuck to the ground. She wants to fold herself over until she starts growing inside out. She does not want to run away, she wants to run home.

Across the table, Mum is staring at her. She will find a way to corner Lona before the afternoon is over. She has been calling every few nights to ask how Lona is going, to ask what her plans are for the rest of the year. Dad always seems to be standing right beside Mum while she's speaking, impatiently jockeying for the phone. He takes the first opportunity he can get to nick it and start telling Lona for the hundredth time that she should be watching *The Crown*. Doing his best Claire Foy doing her best the Queen: one does not wish to badger one's daughter, but one will do so until she heeds one's recommendation.

Lona misses living with her parents so much it's ridiculous. But here, now, she can't think of anything to say to them. She's afraid to lift her eyes from her plate.

Jodie yacks on and on about grabbing the bull by the horns and—contradictorily, in Lona's opinion—getting the hell away from the bulls during the Pamplona Bull Run.

'You are *not* running with the bulls, Jode,' Pat says.

Jodie rolls her eyes. 'I'm not saying I was going to. But it *is* meant to be a life-altering experience. Like, it'll *change your life*.'

Lona doesn't realise she's pulling a face until she looks up and sees it mirrored by the one Mum is wearing. Their eyes catch and their lips fold in unison, quieting their laughter with a shared grimace.

The thing about trolleys

The thing about trolleys is they're like the Magic Pudding. By the time Lona's wheeled one stack back into the supermarket, there are already several more trolleys jammed into the collection point. And regardless of the clearly demarcated bays for BIG TROLLEYS and SMALL TROLLEYS, it is always an absolute shit show.

As she returns to gather a new stack, she finds a woman shoving what is clearly a BIG TROLLEY into the SMALL TROLLEY depository. Usually, since she avoids conflict at all costs, and is in fact paid to be helpful in a subservient, unintimidating kind of way, she would simply rearrange the trolleys herself once the woman was gone. She would wish plague and petulance on the woman's entire family only under her breath. But the thing about trolley duty is that there is a lot of time to think about things and what Lona has been thinking about is *The Magic Pudding*, that supposedly esteemed classic of Australian children's literature. Lona has been considering how messed up it is that all those humans and bushland creatures used to eat an animate pudding, regardless of whether it would grow back or not.

'That's not the right stack,' Lona finds herself telling the woman.

The woman looks around with a slight look of concern on her face until she sees that Lona is a young woman, and she remembers that she is not required to take young women seriously or respect their authority or their humanity.

'The other one is blocked with the wrong trolley,' the woman says defiantly, pointing to a SMALL TROLLEY in the BIG TROLLEY depository.

'And so you couldn't take that out and put it in the other stack instead?' Lona demands.

'I'm in a hurry,' the woman says, already starting to walk away. 'It's your job, isn't it?'

'A curse on all your kin!' Lona yells after her, and the woman starts to jog, shooting an unsettled glance over her shoulder. 'A biblical frog storm unto your home! Leeches, locusts—'

'Kim!'

Lona spots Greg, the manager of trolleys, striding across the car park.

'And that was *Macbeth*, act four, scene seven,' she calls quickly after the woman. 'Next time we'll do *The Merchant of Venice*, all right? Or maybe some Arthur Miller for a change? *Death of a Salesman*? "Oh, Biff, football football don't you want to be like your daddy...American Dream... shattered...masculinity...under...imminent threat..."'

Greg squeezes his eyes at her suspiciously. 'What's going on here? There are trolleys everywhere. Come on, fix it up.'

The staffroom

Lona gets her bag out of her locker. Tony, Alan and Yasmin are sitting at the table in the staffroom. Alan is attempting to contribute to the conversation despite having never read the book Tony and Yasmin are discussing.

Yasmin says, 'I can't believe you don't like Thadius.'

Tony says, 'He's clearly working with the Shadow Queen.'

Alan says, 'Doesn't he get killed in the second season?'

Yasmin gives him a withering look. 'We're talking about the books. They're, like, completely different and *better* than the series.'

Lona checks her phone and sees she's got four missed calls from Pat. 'Oh, shit,' she says, remembering instantly she'd said she would fill in at Planet Skate on Tuesdays while Jodie is overseas. She doesn't ring up voicemail to listen to the messages. She doesn't want to hear Pat being properly disappointed in her.

She sends a text like a coward:

I am so sorry Pat. I completely forgot and I feel so bad. Let me make it up to you. I'll work anytime you need, just let me know so I can square it with Coles. Lona.

She is worried that this will be it for Planet Skate. Pat has already been hinting that she should quit, seeing as she's hardly available for shifts. It wouldn't be the worst thing. But Lona would miss it. The laps at the end of the night at least.

Pat replies:

Ok

Pat always replies just: Ok. It usually makes Lona laugh. Right now she feels shredded by the guilt. There's a series of messages from Tab too:

are you still alive lone?

heeeelllooo

reply to me or i shall spontaneously combust

They have plans, tomorrow or the day after. Or they will, if Lona ever confirms. She should confirm. She should do that right now.

Another message comes through as she is staring at the screen:

ground control to major lone

commencing lockdown engine on

the papers want to know whos skirts you wear

Lona laughs out loud, forgetting for a moment about Pat, and the trolleys and about the fact Thadius is clearly an agent for the Mountain Queen, not the Shadow Queen, and how come no one else seems to realise that?

She messages Tab:

What are we doing and when are we doing it?

Kmart

Tab picks up an orange, long-sleeved t-shirt and asks, 'Will this work?' She drapes it over the front of her torso, checking the length of the arms.

'Yeah, sure,' Lona says dazedly. They have been at Chadstone Shopping Centre for almost three hours, and

Lona's brain has been reduced to a mush specifically formulated by ambient music and a lack of fresh air.

'I want Violet here,' Tab indicates, waving a hand over her chest. 'And then: I DON'T GIVE A DAME printed over it.'

Lona takes the t-shirt from her. She has promised to make her friend a *Downton Abbey* top. She is hoping that painstakingly cutting out Maggie Smith's face with a scalpel will imbue her life with the acute sense of purpose it is currently lacking.

She has not pointed out to Tab that her t-shirt concept makes no sense, and that Violet Crawley is a dowager countess, not a dame like Maggie Smith. She has also not admitted she is yet to be able to stencil a face that looks like a face instead of a smiling blob. She will let those fun revelations emerge with time.

Tab checks the price tag. 'Four dollars!' she exclaims. 'I don't know if I can wear a top that has so clearly screwed someone over at some point. I mean, *god*, *some*one's not getting paid properly.'

She makes no move to translate her moral indignation into the actual, physical act of putting the top back onto the shelf. Both friends accept her outrage as enough, considering their fiscal insecurity and also their laziness.

They continue to wander around Kmart for no purpose other than: they are here, and so is it. Tab remembers she needs some tights and while she is choosing between opaque and semi-opaque and semi-sheer and sheer-opaque,

Lona finds herself staring at a headless, legless mannequin in a mostly crotchless pair of underwear and matching lace bra.

Lona has not bought a new bra since she was seventeen. They do not have to work very hard to hold her in place. She has never needed underwire and she has never wanted lace. She has two beige bras and one black. She tends to wear the black one whenever it's likely George will be seeing it because she has gathered from television that beige bras do not exist in the same universe as sex.

Tab finds her staring at the mannequin and tilts her head. 'Sex robot, très chic.'

Lona doesn't know how to ask the question she wants to ask. She is imagining herself in the sex robot ensemble. She is imagining George touching her in the sex robot ensemble. She is then considering the grossness of wrapping women's body parts individually only for the sake of being opened and accessed.

'Do you...' She looks at the neatly folded piles of see-through undies on the table. 'Should I...'

But she doesn't get the question out, and Lona is relieved when Tab drifts over to the back wall where there are racks of high-waisted, cotton undergarments. The kind that Lona's mum wears. Tab says, 'This is exactly what I need. I'm so sick of wearing things around my hips. I'm migrating north, baby!'

Lona is pretty sure that Tab doesn't wear crotchless underwear. That the very prospect offends her particular brand of feminism. Lona is unsure what her own particular brand of feminism is, when it's detached from Tab's.

She finds the thought of George finding her sexy sexy. But the thought of wearing something just because a man will find it sexy is complicatedly icky. She is also dubious about the functionality of crotchless undies. It's not like they're everyday wear. But she is dubious about lace and pale pink and little love-hearts and anything that is aggressively feminine anyway. She cannot work out whether that means she has rejected the patriarchy or internalised it.

She follows Tab to the checkout, glancing one last time at the headless, legless mannequin with the ample-but-not-too-ample bosom and the flat stomach.

And she wonders: why is that a thing I'm trying to be.

The Astor Theatre

She's already in her dressing gown when George arrives. 'They're showing a double bill of *Spirited Away* and *Howl's Moving Castle* at the Astor tonight,' he tells her. 'I got us tickets.'

This would be sweet if it wasn't for three factors:

1) Lona is already in her dressing gown
2) Lona wants to remain in her dressing gown
3) Lona is still terrified of No-Face, a decade and a half after Mum borrowed *Spirited Away* from the video store because she was sick and tired of Lona making her watch *Cinderella 2* every Friday night

'Oh,' Lona says. 'I thought we were just going out for dinner.'

Lona had been hoping to downgrade *going out* for dinner, to the much more luxurious *staying in and making strangers bring tacos* for dinner. She has the pressing tingle of an almost-headache just above her left eyebrow.

She does not want to go out to stare at a gigantic wall of light and colour. She wants to stare at the small box of light and colour on their TV stand until she feels sick from nausea, and then she wants to go to bed.

'Come on,' George says. 'It's just the Astor. It's not that far.'

But the getting out of the house is the hard thing. The making herself the person she is for everyone else is the painful thing. Lona opens her mouth to explain, but she doesn't know how. George would be hurt if he thought she was hiding some of herself from him. He understands there are masks she wears, for friends, for family, for strangers, but he wouldn't understand the one she wears for him.

He would be hurt by her need to hoard herself for herself. The sad, restless Lona. The weak Lona. The Lona that she folds away for when no one else is around, keeping all the gory insides out of sight. He would say: give it to me, all of it, and I'll help. But Lona doesn't want him handling those parts. Those parts are hers.

She wanted to be alone tonight, but she was willing to concede dinner. She is fumbling for a way to say: I want you, but I don't want you now.

She can't find a way to make them both happy and so she says, 'All right, just let me get dressed.'

At the dinner table

Lona finds herself torn between a deep longing to go home for dinner and a fear of talking to her parents about her decisions in life. In the end, the prospect of a meal that isn't either pesto pasta or kale salad wins out.

She nearly falls asleep on the train and almost misses her station. She gets through the doors just as they are closing automatically, her outstretched limbs presenting an obstacle that the mechanism doesn't expect. There's a moment when it's almost as if they're going to crush her, then the system relents and the doors go slack.

She touches off with her travel card and is told she has -$1.37 on her MYKI. She has a couple of dollars of change in her wallet that will get her back to Carnegie.

It's a fifteen-minute walk to her parents' house. She's done it so many times she doesn't have to think about it, just lets her feet carry her under the overpass and down along the golf course. It's bright still, and warm.

Lona is feeling shit about things, both generally and specifically. (The stiffness in her shoulders, the twitch in her right eye, the amorphous shape of her future, the removal of *Sliding Doors* from Netflix.) She is attempting to see past this afternoon to a time when she doesn't feel shit about things, neither generally nor specifically. It shouldn't be hard, but it is.

At home, Mum makes gin and tonics. Dad has just signed up for Spotify Premium and, as Lona feared he one day would, he has discovered *Hamilton*. She knows she will spend a good portion of the next five years listening to him rap about American political history.

Lona sits in the armchair opposite the one that Grandpa used to sit in. It was only Grandpa's for the few months that he lived here, but Lona can't stop seeing it now as: Grandpa's chair.

Mum attempts to chat to her from the kitchen. She finally cracks it and demands that Dad turn down the music. The talk that follows is small: weather, neighbours, work. Lona is wary of the impersonal nature of these inquiries. All it tells her is the meaty stuff is still on its way.

She is tired. Her phone is tired too. It's almost run out of charge and she is eagerly anticipating the time when she can no longer be held responsible for not replying to the nice and cosmically pointless things people have messaged her.

At the dinner table, the physical and metaphorical knives come out. Mum asks if Lona has been in to see Grandpa recently. When Lona says no, her parents share a look. They tell her something she already knows along the lines of: family = forevs = more important than binge-watching televisual sci-fi.

Mum asks whether she's thought about going back to uni. Lona shrugs non-committedly. The prospect of studying art is sickening to Lona. The prospect of studying anything else is horrific.

She understands: her parents have lived their lives the way they have so that she can live her life the way they planned. She is the one who is screwing it up. She is the piano dropping through all the levels of that building in *The Aristocats*. She is breaking everything that is trying to support her.

On the bright side: the baked salmon is nice.

Late one evening

Tab calls late one evening. She's driving around aimlessly and she wonders if Lona might want to go for a ride. Lona says yes because the proposed activity requires minimal effort beyond sitting up and staying awake. Tab texts when she's idling out front in her dad's white sedan:

here

Lona goes out and gets into the car. She's in her pyjamas and slippers. She has pulled on a hoodie for decency's sake. 'What's up?' she asks.

Tab is not in a talking mood. She is in a driving mood and so she drives. They don't go anywhere. Or rather: they don't go anywhere in particular. Lona understands objectively that everywhere is somewhere, even the streets they drive along that look like every other street. Every house has someone or something in it, a person who thinks and feels and worries and wonders, a person with a name and a resolute belief in their own distinct personhood. But this is too great and cascading a reality to comprehend fully without having to clutch the sides of her head, so what happens is: she doesn't think about it too long.

Tab's phone screen lights up and so does the console it's jammed in. Her mother is calling. Tab and her mother do things like fight with each other and possibly actually mean the things they say. Lona guesses that it's one of those nights. She doesn't have any words of wisdom. She only has words she's heard on television and read in books. She does what she knows how to do: be there. She puts the radio on something they both kind of like and they both kind of sing along.

Tab says, 'You want a McFlurry?'

She takes them to one of the many Macca's on North Road. Tab gets Oreo for herself and M&Ms for Lona. They sit in the car with the cabin light on, parked facing out over the intersection with its signals going green orange red. Lona switches the music to the Florence + the Machine CD that's in the player. It's the recent one. The softer than usual one.

'Remember Jack Kyneton at school camp?' Tab asks.

'Shitting his pants?' Lona asks.

'Yeah, wonder what he's up to.'

Lona digs out all her M&Ms before their colours marble through the soft serve. Her head's aching a bit from the cold. There's a solitary car waiting at the intersection. A green people mover. The light stays red and it just sits there, even though there are no cars coming through from the other direction.

'I wanted to ask him out,' Tab says. 'But I didn't know whether it was because I felt sorry for him or because I actually liked him. I have a thing for the underdog, you know. It's almost pathological. I watch the footy with Nick and I can't help going for whoever's losing, and then if they start winning, I switch sides.'

Lona looks across at her friend. 'Are you saying you only hang out with me because I'm a loser?'

Tab laughs. 'I'm *saying* that I don't know if I actually want any of the things I think I want. I'm *saying*—'

There's a loud, tearing screech: the sound of metal shredding through metal, the sound of glass smashing into a hundred million pieces. Lona's McFlurry jumps in her hands and her head snaps back to the intersection. There are two cars now, mashed into one another, the green people mover pushed halfway across the line. The green signal insists that it's time to go. It is ignorant to the impossibility of go. The exhaust is billowing out the back of the other car. It has its nose buried in the passenger side of the people mover, devouring it. Lona cannot remember if there was a passenger in the passenger side.

'Oh, shit,' she says, somewhat belatedly.

Tab is already opening the door and getting out. Lona follows her in an uneven walk-run, like one leg is trying to hold her back. There's a hubcap in the gutter. The road crunches with broken glass like the dance floor of a seedy nightclub. Lona catches up to Tab, who's standing dumb at the pedestrian crossing like she needs to be told: walk. The strip of shops up the road is lit up, but nothing's stirred yet. It feels apocalyptic, like it's just the night and them. Lona is still holding her McFlurry.

They can't see anything. There are airbags exploded in each car, making it look like they're full of raw dough. Lona's brain is associating wildly, grasping for something, anything explicable.

'We need to call an ambulance,' Tab says.

'I don't have my phone,' Lona says. Tab's is back in the console.

The door of the other car is forced open from the inside. The man doing the forcing is pushing at his airbag. He staggers out of the car and there is blood running from his nose. It's split across the bridge. Tab rushes forward, Lona right behind.

'Are you ok?' Tab calls.

The man is bent over. 'Fuck,' he groans. '*Fuck*.' He's older than them, but he's young. Tab reaches for him and he recoils. There's a gash in his forehead, matted with hair. He's concussed and confused. Tab draws back her hand like she's been stung.

There's a thump from the other car, as the woman in the people mover slams her door shut behind her. 'You fucking psycho!' she screams, and suddenly she's in the other driver's face and she lashes out with flat palms into his chest, pushing him back so that he stumbles. She's bleeding from her nose and the corner of her mouth.

'What if I'd had my daughter in the back of the car?' she screams. 'What if my daughter was in there?'

Lona and Tab are motionless. They look at what's left of the empty infant chair in the back seat of the people mover. It's been pushed halfway over the top of the seat in front of it. They look at each other. Lona can't feel her hands around the paper cup. This time when the woman hits the man he loses his balance, and he lands on the asphalt with a soft thud.

'Fuck,' he says dumbly. 'I'm sorry. I'm—*fuck*.' He looks at the palms he used to break his fall. They're studded with glass dust.

The woman glances at Lona and Tab for the first time and her anger snaps into smaller pieces. She's shaking and her voice is brittle when she demands, 'You saw that, right? You saw that he hit me? It was a fucking red light he went through!'

They don't move, don't say anything, don't know how to explain: we weren't looking, we don't know, we believe you but we can't put our hand on a bible or our heart or whatever and swear it.

Tab says, 'Do you want me to get you some water?' and the woman stares at her like she's insane, until finally she says, 'Yes,' dully, and she begins to cry.

Lona says, 'I'll do it,' because she doesn't know what to do here, and Tab's already got an arm around the woman. She walks back to Macca's and only realises she's been scooping the last of her McFlurry into her mouth when her straw hits the bottom of the cup. Several people are pushing out of McDonald's as she walks in. 'Water,' she says, but no one hears her, and it doesn't really matter, because the offer was only ever an excuse to say something instead of nothing, and her eagerness to fulfil it was just a means of being somewhere else.

She watches from the car park as more and more people crowd the intersection. There are cars slowing and stopping. Diners and staff spill out of McDonald's and from the restaurants up the road. The sound of a siren is dull in the distance, and then seemingly instantly close and wailing. The red and blue lights are thrown across Tab's back as she crouches beside the man, one arm on his shoulder.

Lona turns around and there's someone she doesn't know standing there. 'Did you see it happen?' they ask.

She glimpses the flash of foil shock blankets as they are wrapped around the drivers. A paramedic offers one to Tab and Tab waves a hand. She points to Lona in the car park, or probably more likely to her car that's still sitting there, doors flung open.

A police officer is setting up cones around the cars and there is someone sweeping up the debris. It's over, basically.

Lona goes to wait by Tab's car.

Talk about it

Lona spends the night at her parents' place. She sleeps in Ben's old room in Ben's old bed. In the morning she eats a

132

bowl of Nutri-Grain.

George calls and he hasn't heard, which means that Nick hasn't heard, which means that Tab hasn't told him yet. Lona says, 'We witnessed a car crash last night.' The words are mechanical and not exactly true, considering Lona was looking at Tab and Tab was looking at Lona when it happened, and what they witnessed was technically: cars crashed. George is concerned, which Lona is beginning to realise is his modus operandi.

'You need to talk about it?' he asks.

There are many things Lona needs:

a) a good sleep

b) a future

c) a spine

There are many things Lona wants:

a) the new Jay Kristoff book

b) Mum's spaghetti bolognese without having to ask for it

c) a slow, exploratory fuck

What she neither needs nor wants is to talk about it.

'Let's go out tonight,' she suggests.

This proposition coming from Lona is a blue moon, a dark horse, a Tasmanian tiger. It's such a shock, George doesn't know what to say. 'Ok,' he says warily. 'If that's what you want.'

When she hangs up, she sends a message to Tab:

Hey (SMILING FACE) how are you feeling? Crazy night, am I right?

She doesn't get a response, which is ok, because she wouldn't know what to do with one anyway. She lies on the couch and stares at the crack in the ceiling that always cracks no matter how many times Dad paints over it, and she wishes she were more motivated in life.

Rehab

Grandpa is moved to the rehab centre at Caulfield Hospital. He has been told he is going to have to use a wheelchair. He is being given rehab of the body so that he can adjust to this reality. He is not being given rehab of the mind, even though Lona thinks this is probably equally crucial seeing as he has spent 86 years of his life having legs that functioned, and now he has legs that have to be lifted by arms like they're some cumbersome, malignant growth. Lona goes in on Tuesdays, when she has the afternoon off from Coles.

Grandpa is sometimes out of bed when she arrives at 3 p.m., but a lot of the time he's not. 'I'm exhausted today,' he tells her. Lona tries not to feel annoyed at him for not trying harder with the rehab. She says, 'Once you get the hang of the wheelchair, you'll be able to get around a lot faster than you did with the walker.'

'It's not as easy as it looks,' he says. He often does rounds of the hospital corridor in the mornings. He is proud when he can manage two.

Lona sits down in the wheelchair. She takes off the gel cushion that's meant to stop sores from forming and wheels this way and that around the room. She imagines that the patients in the other beds think she is: just darling. That they are bemused by her blue hair, and impressed with her attentiveness to her grandfather. In reality, they watch their televisions and breathe through their mouths and couldn't care less. Grandpa raises an arm. The skin hangs from the bone in a way that makes it obvious that it is skin hanging from bone. 'Stop mucking around,' he says. Lona feels the muscles working in her arms. Her bones are nowhere in sight. She gets up and wheels the chair back over, puts the cushion back on. Grandpa presses a button on his remote control so that the mattress lifts his head slightly and he can see her properly.

She wants Grandpa to get better because she likes Grandpa better when he's not in hospital. This is horrible, and this is true.

'You'll be home soon,' she says. 'In no time.'

She gets out her book and sits on the corner of the bed, starts reading aloud. It's a story about an old man looking back on a love affair he had in his youth. The concepts examined are: the nature of time, the subjectivity of recollection, the weight of knowledge. The male gaze is strong, or in other words: it's a literary novella. It's written so beautifully that Lona forgives it, over and over, hand on her heart.

When she folds down the corner of the page and closes the book, Grandpa has this look on his face like he's not been listening for a long time now. Maybe it was the wrong story. An unnecessary story for a man who is forced to look back because he can barely see ahead of himself. Who can't even walk those few steps needed to get close enough to what's out of focus. He presses another button on his remote that raises his knees for him. Lona is displaced from the end of the bed.

She stands up, says, 'I'll see you next week.'

Tab calls

Tab calls around 10.30 p.m. and wants to talk. She wants to talk but she doesn't know what to talk about. Lona guesses she's been fighting with her mum again. Tab says, 'That was crazy.'

Lona agrees, even though she doesn't know what they're discussing.

'I'm so glad they were both ok,' Tab says.

'Oh, yeah,' Lona agrees, comprehending.

'I keep thinking,' Tab says. Lona waits to hear what Tab keeps thinking, but it seems that the sentence ends there.

Lona tries to discuss a book they've both just read. Tab mmms. She says, 'I was speaking in class the other day and I couldn't stop, I was just talking, talking, talking and the whole time I was thinking: who's talking, who is this. Everyone thinks I'm this bright, happy person.'

'That's what the girl in the book feels like,' Lona says eagerly. 'Like when she goes to that party with Angelo. The abstracted self thing.'

Tab does not marvel at the cosmic synchronicity of this

coincidence. 'The abstracted self thing,' she repeats.

'Yeah, it's a trope.'

'A trope.'

'Like alienation in coming-of-age narratives. Like, what's more abstracting: abstraction or being abstracted from abstraction.'

Tab doesn't say anything for a while and when she does it's like she's skipped ahead. 'One size fits all,' she says.

Tab does not seem to be enjoying the conversation, but she resists Lona's attempts to let it die a painless death. Lona does the legwork. Lona is not used to doing the legwork. 'Let's see a movie tomorrow,' she suggests. She expects Tab to say no, but Tab says yes.

'Yes,' Tab says. 'All right.'

They hang up without having worked out where they're going or what they're seeing. Lona can't remember the last time Tab was like this. She realises: Tab has never been like this.

At the movies

The film they see has been out for weeks, so there are only two other people in the cinema. It's a cavernous theatre, rows and rows of empty chairs like a flood of red blood cells. Lona and Tab sit with their feet up on the seats in front of them and there's the distinct sense: it's us against the world.

The movie is loud and senseless. Lona waits for Tab's usual commentary, the sarcastic remarks and genuine questions about what's that actor been in and is that his girlfriend or the woman from the bank that usually populate any viewing and have infuriated Lona for years. But the most she gets is a murmured: how long did you say this goes for?

Tab's phone rings and she walks up to the back row to take the call. Lona glances back at her. Tab's hair is pulled back into a scraggly bun. She is wearing ugg boots and a long, floral skirt. She chews on the edge of her thumbnail. When Lona turns back to the screen she sees the other two people moving around on the carpet directly below the projection. They are dancing. She realises that they are girls, only just teenagers. One of them cartwheels, the other claps. Their laughter is like water moving through a maze of pipes. The music from the film cuts out as the scene switches, but they reach out for each other's hands so that they can wash the dishes dry the dishes turn the dishes over.

Tab sits back down beside Lona. She doesn't tell Lona who she was speaking to. Lona doesn't ask. Lona doesn't know what this feeling is, the one in her gut that makes her feel sick and impatient. She doesn't know why Tab isn't telling her what's wrong when Tab always tells her what's wrong.

The girls down the front of the cinema are taking selfies. The flash on the phone is bright white and stabs a hole through Lona's vision. She blinks until it is gone.

Tab elbows Lona. 'What's that actor been in?' she asks.

Lona saddles her feelings so that she can sit on them

without being thrown off. She says, 'The film we watched where the woman with the split personality disorder thought one of her personalities murdered her husband's lover but it turned out that her husband's lover was one of her personalities. He was the best friend.'

Tab nods. 'Ah, of course.'

Indisputable maths

It's March before Lona finally facilitates the being of George and her parents in the same room at the same time.

Dad's having a birthday lunch at home, and Lona drops in a simple request: can George come. Her parents' enthusiasm is deliberately muted, because they don't want to scare her back into being the daughter no one wants: the smart, independent, single daughter.

She is taking this opportunity to introduce George to her parents because lunch is a safe meal. The maths is indisputable:

Lunch = less alcohol = less regret

Lunch can also be left at pretty much anytime, whereas with dinner there's always the pressure to: stay until the night is over. No one ever ends up playing Pictionary at a lunch party. For that, humanity is grateful.

George stays over at Lona's the night before Dad's birthday. 'So I finally get to meet the Wallaces,' he says.

'You know it's me not you, right?' she says.

'It's ok. I know you're ashamed of me. I've come to terms with the fact I'm probably actually just your side piece.'

They are watching television and her head is in his lap and she looks up at him to make sure he is smiling. She can tell he's joking, and she knows he's fine and they're fine, and it will all be fine, but she's not entirely emotionally inept. She knows he wouldn't say it if he wasn't trying to make it funny not hurt.

She sits up and he says, 'You've got your serious face on.'

She says, 'I want to explain it to you.'

'You don't need to explain it to me.' The television screen freezes on Hopper and Eleven. Lona has paused *Stranger Things*. George says, 'Shit, ok, I didn't realise it was *that* serious.'

She leans forward to kiss him. 'I love you just for that.'

'For what?'

'For noticing things about me and liking them.' She stares at him. Up close she can see his pores and the dry skin at the edge of his mouth. 'It's not that I didn't want you to meet my parents,' she insists. 'It's just... I know...I know that me being with you will make them happier than anything else I could do, or could want to do.'

He shakes his head instantly. 'That's ridiculous.'

'It's not,' she says. 'I know you won't get this, but...'

'It's not that I don't get it,' he interrupts. 'I get what you're trying to say.'

She sits back on her heels, bristling. 'No, you don't.' She squeezes her fists, and she knows she's not angry at him, she's not even angry at her parents, she's angry at: the way things are. But George is here and easier to argue with than a societal structure. 'All the things *I* want and *I* want to do will not make them as happy as me being in a stable relationship or being married or having kids. And I'm not saying I don't want those things—I'm not saying I do. I'm just saying fuck that.'

'It's the same for me,' he says.

'No, it's not,' she says, frustrated. 'You know, I sometimes thought I'd never be in a relationship. I didn't care, but everyone else did.'

'Well, what do you want me to do? Not be with you? Just so you can make some sort of statement?' He gets up and gets the half-drunk bottle of rosé from the kitchen bench. 'What the hell is the point in that? Would that make you happy?'

She rolls her eyes, looks back at the TV. If she cut her hair really short, she reckons it'd look like Eleven's. She wonders what George would think. Fuck what George would think.

He says, 'Are you listening to me or have you decided the conversation is over?' He refills her glass, then his. When he sits back on the couch she can feel the sting of his eyes on the side of her face.

The male gaze. The thing she always wanted, despised, coveted.

'I can never say exactly what I mean,' she says, and like all deeply true things it just sounds like shit.

He brushes a thumb over the inside of her wrist. 'I'm sorry.'

Her voice is an empty chamber. 'I'm sorry too.'

Each other's arms

They sleep in each other's arms and it's about 98 per cent less romantic than it sounds. He has to bend his tall body to fit in her bed, and she knows it's uncomfortable for him, and she knows that he wishes she'd get a bigger bed, but part of her wants him to say, 'Ok, I'm sleeping on the couch,' and for it not to be a big deal.

It'd be pointless trying to explain to him that buying a bigger bed had always seemed unnecessary and overly optimistic to her. That she hadn't expected him. That changing things for his sake makes her feel weak. It'd be like talking to him about her parents. He's understanding but he doesn't understand.

She likes it when he holds her and they talk with their faces close, but she can't sleep like that. She's too aware of him, too possessed by him and his self and the space he fills in space that has always been just hers. She is awake for long hours and then she is asleep. In the morning, she's on her own. George gets up early, he can't help it.

He makes the most of having to watch the TV with the volume down and binges an intense Scandinavian crime show on Netflix. Lona likes knowing that he is just on the other side of the room divider. She lies in her bed by herself and she loves him dearly.

White people

Lona rings the doorbell because she is no longer sure whether she should use her keys or not. Harriet answers, which makes Lona irrationally irritable.

By way of introduction, she says, 'George, this is not a member of my family,' or more likely she says something politer and less true.

Everyone else is in the kitchen. Lona has not told her parents anything about George. Mum and Dad turn around with expectant faces, and there's an infinitesimal flash of surprise when they clock George. It's just a small: this boy is not white. Mum and Dad are not racist, they are simply white people who assumed their white daughter was bringing home a white boy. White people will do that. Any confusion is gone in a split second. 'George,' Mum says. 'Lovely to meet you.'

Dad shakes his hand, as does Ben. Lona can glimpse the patriarchy in the air sealed by their palms. George accepts the beer he is offered. He glances sideways at Lona with a look that says: easy peasy. Last night's argument is still sitting in Lona's joints, making it hard for her to relax. She watches the way George charms her parents and another familiar feeling hits her: that in their enjoyment of each other's company, her presence is becoming redundant with all of the people she loves.

Do-It-Yourself bread rolls

Dad's favourite meal is Do-It-Yourself bread rolls. This

involves serving guests the ingredients for a sandwich and making them make it themselves. Lona can tell that George is fascinated by this insight into the white, middle-class mind. He makes himself a ham-and-cheese focaccia and tells Lona's parents the things he knows parents love hearing: that he studies medicine, that he plays cello, that he gets on well with his brothers. He seems slightly puzzled that Lona's parents don't already know these things. He is attempting to gauge how much Lona has told them. He is failing to ascertain the relevant data, as the information is not only off the chart, but the chart simply does not exist.

'I'm not sure if Lona told you, but when we played at the Toff last week—'

'Played?' Dad interrupts.

'Yeah, Hello Hello, my band—'

'Your band?' Ben says.

'Hello Hello?' Harriet chimes in. 'I think I heard you guys on Triple J Unearthed a while ago.'

George is attempting to be modest, but he's glowing so much Lona feels compelled to pull out a Geiger counter. 'Yeah, as I was saying, at the Toff we were talking to Nick—Tab's boyfriend—and—'

Mum stares at Lona. 'Tab has a boyfriend?'

This stops George right in his tracks, his mouth halfway open, and there's silence all around the table. Everyone's looking at Lona. Lona is looking at her pane di casa roll. 'Um,' she says. 'Didn't I mention that?'

Pictures of The Greatest Band Humanly Possible

George stares at the pictures of The Greatest Band Humanly Possible plastered to the wall above where Lona's bed used to be. 'You reckon I should cut my hair like that?' he jokes, pointing at a particularly lush shot of the lead singer's bowl cut.

Lona is sitting on her desk chair, slowly swivelling from side to side. It's strange having a boy in her room. Stranger still that's he's standing right where her bed used to be. He slides his hands into his pockets. 'Don't you tell your parents anything?'

She shrugs. 'I tell them things. Just not...all things.'

'I don't understand what the big deal is.'

She shrugs again. 'I don't understand what the big deal is if I don't.'

He looks at her uncomprehendingly. 'Because that's what you do with the people in your life. You share things with them. You tell them things.'

'I think that's one of humanity's greatest errors.' She's approximately sixty per cent joking. 'I'm sorry. I promise I'll give them a beat-by-beat review of every gig you play from now on.'

He doesn't say anything for a bit. 'It really doesn't matter to you, does it?' he says finally.

'Are we talking hypothetically, historically or... allegorically?' She's trying to make him smile, but he's not smiling. 'George, I love you and I love my parents. I just don't feel the need to tell everyone everything all the time.

In fact, I prefer to tell people nothing.'

He stares at her.

'What?'

'Who do you talk to?' he asks softly.

'You. Tab.'

'About everything?'

She shakes her head.

He leans back against the wall, pancaking the poor band. 'Why not?'

She sucks her bottom lip, can't explain it, can never explain it. The need to hoard herself for herself. She doesn't feel like herself in this conversation. Has forgotten which self she's trying to be. She opens her mouth but she can't think of anything. Her eyes skit and skate until they land on the polaroids blu-tacked to her wardrobe. Snaps of Tab and accidental snaps of bare walls and kitchen tiles. Between them, illustrations ripped out of magazines, postcards of artworks and ripply jet-cartridge prints of old photography projects. A handful of self-portraits.

All she's ever wanted to say, all she's ever wanted to howl. Art like artillery, like an act of self-surgery. Art makes it easy to be brave, makes it easy to rage and strut and feel. It's all there, if he would just *look*.

Art like articulation. Like screaming soundlessly to be heard.

Old Kim

Old Kim corners Lona by the dumpsters round the back

of Coles. 'I've got a favour to ask you, darl,' Old Kim says. This is an ominous start to a conversation, so Lona squints, 'Oh, yeah?'

'I was hoping you could cover my Saturday morning shift,' Old Kim says.

This coming Saturday is the first Saturday Lona has had off in months. She is looking forward to turning her alarm off. She is looking forward to a Friday night spent up till the wee hours with Graham Norton and Ellen Page.

In lieu of a better excuse, Lona goes with: 'Ummm...'

Old Kim nods. 'My own fault, of course. Saw a flyer for an art class and signed myself up, an impulse thing. Beginner's watercolour at the CAE. I always wanted to be Beatrix Potter when I was a girl.'

'Oh,' Lona says.

'It's a six-week course. Worst comes to worst I could miss the first one.' She shrugs like she's already accepted it. There's no grievance, no resentment in the way she claps a hand on Lona's shoulder. 'But how are you doing out here, darl? I hardly see you these days. Do you always take your break out here?'

Lona has got a fist full of half-eaten muesli bar. She is crouched on a step where the smokers smoke. She has never smoked aside from that time with Mr Higgins. She wants to look like the kind of person who smokes. There's something about it: the back step, the dumpsters, the same sort of muesli bar day after day. She's been waiting for someone to find her like that.

'It's all right,' she says.

Old Kim has brought a homemade ham and cheese sandwich for her lunch break. It's in a sandwich box, the kind Lona's mother used to pack her for school. Old Kim sits down beside Lona and eats. Lona knows that the longer she stays there, the more likely it is she is going to offer to take the shift. There's an inevitability about it. Lona is not generally a shit person. Only sometimes.

'How are Jack and Robbie?' she asks.

Old Kim rolls her eyes. 'Boys will be boys.'

Lona nods. After a bit she frowns. 'What does that mean?' she asks.

Old Kim looks at her, then barks a laugh. 'Who knows?'

Jack and Robbie still live at home with Old Kim, even though they're both in their thirties. Her husband went to the 7-Eleven for a Four'n Twenty pie fifteen years ago and hasn't been heard from since. Old Kim has no time for people who mumble and no time for posturing. Her hair looks like it's never seen conditioner. She's had her red Coles vest since she was at least two sizes smaller. She doesn't laugh if something's not funny, not like Lona, whose laughter is an involuntary stutter when she feels uncomfortable. Old Kim stares at people until they say something that is actually worth being said.

'I'll cover the shift,' Lona says.

'Thanks, darl,' Old Kim says through a mouthful. 'I owe you one.'

Enter message here

Lona messages Tab. The words sit on the screen in the palm of her hand:

Hey what's up?

They sit there and they don't do anything. It stuns Lona suddenly that she expects the tapping of fingers onto a piece of glass and plastic to mean anything to anyone. She waits for a reply, for pixels to show up on her palm in the formation of sentiments she wants to read. Something easy like:

not much

how bout you?

Or better, something warm and eager like:

you me hot chips now

All she gets is a white box that advises her to enter message here. She puts her phone on the coffee table while she watches *Buffy*. She can't concentrate. She finds the phone in her hands without consciously reaching for it. She presses the screen and it lights up and not only has Tab not messaged her, but no one else has either. She is the definition of sitting by the phone, except that now the phone sits with her wherever she goes, tucked into the inner pocket of her jacket.

Tab continues to not-reply. It's been two weeks since the night at Macca's. Lona has already told everyone she knows about it. No one seems to think it's that interesting, probably because no one died.

Lona finds that in this uselessly, preposterously

149

connected world, Tab's silence is astoundingly abrasive.

Tab's mother

Lona calls Tab at home, which she hasn't done in a long time. She has to rack her brain for the landline, but the string of numbers is still there, snagged on memories of long phone conversations about *Inkheart* and *Neighbours* before they switched to mobiles for good. Tab's mother picks up. She tells Lona that Tab is in the Dandenongs for the week.

'With Nick?' Lona asks, instantly peeved that she's been left out of the loop.

'No, by herself,' Linda says.

Lona cannot keep the surprise out of her voice. 'What's she doing?'

'You know Tab,' Linda says wearily.

Lona does know Tab. She knows that Tab loves the mountains and trees that are a hundred people tall. She knows that Tab has always dreamed about running away to a cabin in the woods to get away from everything. The dream has always stung Lona very slightly every time Tab brings it up because it's in the everything that Tab wants to get away from that Lona exists.

'I'm worried,' Linda says. Lona wishes she hadn't said that because she doesn't want to be confided in. She doesn't want to be treated like an adult who is capable of hearing her best friend's mother talk about her daughter like she is a problem. 'Has she said anything to you, Lona?

About why she's struggling at uni?'

The question strikes Lona dumb. This is the first she has heard of it.

Linda sighs. 'Last year when she failed those two units I thought it was just an adjustment period. This year... well, it shouldn't take so long.'

There's a faint whistling in Lona's ears, like the air rushing around a falling object. 'Tell her to call me if you hear from her,' she blurts. 'Thanks Linda.' The goodbye tumbles out of her mouth, half of the words on top of each other. She hangs up.

A pub in Northcote

The information that Lona receives is that someone George knows is turning 21. Or possibly she receives more information than that, but that is all that sticks with her. To celebrate, drinks are being had in a pub in Northcote. Nick gives Lona and George a lift. Nick does not seem to know any more about what is happening with Tab than Lona does.

'She's just getting some fresh air,' he says.

Lona spends the car ride there steeling herself for prolonged exposure to other people. 'You'll finally get to meet the gang,' George says. She cannot remember what gang he is referring to and it is far too late to ask him to clarify. She's met the band and his friends from the music faculty. It must be medicine. But Nick's invited. So the soccer team? School?

Nick parallel parks on High Street. It's somewhere between three and four in the afternoon. 'I'll need to move the car in two hours,' he says, looking at the parking sign. 'Can you guys remind me?'

Because it is of absolutely no consequence to her, Lona instantly forgets. She tucks an arm around George's because she is feeling self-conscious and he is looking particularly hot with his old jeans rolled at the cuffs and his baggy Hawaiian shirt and his The Cars tee.

'You're nervous,' he says, which is not a long shot considering it would be an accurate statement approximately 73 per cent of the time. He squeezes her hand. 'Don't be.'

As if it was that fucking easy.

Inside the pub George and Nick quickly spot their friends. Some of them wave and some of them make the effort to stand up and pat the newcomers' backs. Lona is motioned to and introduced. She pinches the front of her red corduroy skirt and smiles edgily.

George says, 'Come on, let's get a drink.'

She feels instantly better the moment she has something to grip in her fist. George assures her that she is going to fit right in. She wants to stay standing at the bar with him, but he is rudely wanting to spend time with his mates.

Back at the table she is introduced to a Katie and a Pete or potentially a Kathy and a Pat. She's too busy concentrating on being nice to them to absorb their names.

'Lona is an artist,' George says, which surprises her.

She's never described herself as such to him, and he's never actually shown an overwhelming interest in her art. Not that there's been much of it lately.

'Oh, awesome,' his friends say, nodding indulgently.

'Uh, yeah,' Lona says.

'She does event photography too,' George adds. 'Which is sort of how we met—or met again, at least.'

His arm has wound itself over the back her chair. She says, 'But most of my time is spent hanging around a Coles car park.'

'For her job,' George quickly interjects.

Katie prods her drink with a paper straw that has gone soggy. 'I did art in school,' she says.

'So did I!' says Pete.

Unisex bathroom

Lona finds herself wedged between Katie and Nick. They are speaking across her about Rupi Kaur. 'Instagram poets are everything that is wrong with the world,' Katie says, somewhat hyperbolically in Lona's humble opinion.

'Insta influencers are everything that is wrong with the world,' Nick agrees.

Lona thinks she has got the hang of it. 'Instagram is everything wrong with the world,' she says.

The other two stare at her like she is unhinged.

George is on the other side of Nick and he keeps missing the SOS she is Morse coding at him with her eyelids. Blink blink blink. Bliiink bliiink bliiink. Blink blink blink. Nick

153

asks, 'Are you all right, Lona? Is there something in your eye?'

She pulls a pen out of her jacket pocket and doodles on a crumpled napkin. A boy's face which, according to rules of representation, turns into a girl's face the moment she jams a couple of eyelashes in the corners of the eyes. She gives the girl a cute patterned vest and triangular eyebrows. She draws a speech bubble and writes the word: cowabunga.

Katie notices and she says, 'Aw, that's cute.'

All of a sudden, the napkin is being handed around the table. 'Lona is an *artiste*,' someone is narrating for the benefit of others.

Lona wonders when she was upgraded to the sophistication of the French noun. She aims her stoniest look at George, who is trying not to laugh.

She excuses herself to go to the bathroom. This involves half the table standing up to let her out. The toilets are unisex and Lona squats over a urine-splattered seat as she stares at the graffiti and peeling band stickers stuck to the back of the stall door.

There is a Sharpie-scrawled: eat pussy not meat

There is a crossed-out phone number beside: call jez 4 a gud time

There is a: jesus loves you

With an arrow leading to: if your a heteronormative white man

Which someone, Lona is satisfied to see, has corrected

154

to: if *you're* a heteronormative white man

She takes her time washing her hands in the trough sink. She stares at herself in the mirror, comforted somehow by the grimace she receives. Back out in the pub she hovers by the wall for a couple of minutes, watching George be with his friends.

She moves slowly to join them.

In the back seat

On the way home, George switches the radio in Nick's car to Triple J. He doesn't listen to anything else. He has told Lona on multiple occasions that she is a bogan for listening to Triple M, and an old woman for listening to Gold. He is just teasing her, but it sticks pins into her jaw nonetheless.

The boys talk about their friends and Lona wonders for the millionth time where the idea came from that girls are the gossipy ones. Lona learns that Nick used to be involved with Katie. She detests him for daring to be involved with anyone *ever* aside from Tab. He yawns loudly and lengthily, which is always a good sign from the person whose ability to concentrate is determining whether or not the car stays on the road. He and George start to sing along to a song Lona has never heard.

'It'll top the Top 100 for sure,' Nick speculates.

In the back seat, Lona relives the night again and again, fixating on and pulling apart bits that make her cringe. She does not want to be doing this. Her mind, on the other hand, has a sadomasochistic desire to tear itself apart.

'I'm knackered,' Nick says.

Lona nods, picturing herself blanketed on the couch. '*Buffy* then bed.'

George groans. 'Please, I beg of you, no more *Buffy*.'

He is a little bit joking, but mainly serious. George has developed an animosity towards the Vampire Slayer and associated media. He thinks Lona spends more time with Anthony Head than with him. He does not understand that a television show can be a happy place where the world isn't so shit for 43 minutes. He watches bleak crime series and satirical news programs in which a man in a suit sits behind a desk and is cynical about everything within reach.

She says something like, 'I promise it'll be a Spike season,' but she is upset. She does not want to feel embarrassed for wanting to be happy. Especially not at the end of a long afternoon of scrutinising the social and intellectual cues of every new person she meets, trying to work out who she should be with each of them. She bristles at his sweeping of *Buffy* into the category of: guilty pleasure. She detests not only the insinuation, but the concept itself.

It feels like a condemnation of the very thing that makes her her. The obsessive, giddy, impassioned her. The her that cares about something, even if it's a television show. Her jaw feels tight. She is quiet, but she is often quiet, so George has absolutely no idea of the hurt she is

X-ray beaming through the back of his headrest.

A new song comes on and he declares that Father John Misty is a prophet for our age and Lona snaps, 'Ironic misogyny is just as harmful as genuine misogyny.'

He ducks slightly, like he has no idea where that was lobbed from. There's a confused, wounded look on his face that she catches in the side mirror. The satisfaction and regret hit her at the same time.

'You know, I think you're right, Lona,' Nick says.

Oh shut up, she thinks.

Community theatre production

Dad buys two tickets to a community theatre production of *Shrek the Musical*. Astonishingly, Mum does not wish to accompany him, so the ticket is offered to Lona.

Lona and her father are seated two rows from the front. They are close enough to the stage that Lona recognises Sampson's friend Martin through the heavy green face paint. He again demonstrates his penchant for high kicks as he belts out 'I'm a Believer'. Dad has already downloaded the Broadway soundtrack and silently mouths along with the musical numbers.

Lona is pretty sure that she saw the tunic Martin is wearing at Kmart when she was there with Tab. She wishes Tab were here to witness the full glory of the Elsternwick Players Society. She wishes Tab were here.

After the show, Dad insists they hang around in the lobby of the town hall so that he can congratulate the fifteen-year-old kid playing Donkey for providing an exceptional level of professionalism in what was otherwise, he whispers confidentially to Lona, a grade-A shit show on the level of the production of To Kill a Mockingbird the Musical that Lona and Tab participated in at high school. 'Not that you weren't great as Member of Lynch Mob Number Five,' he adds quickly.

Dad believes in the power of positive thought and he believes in Lona. When he asks her how things are going, whilst straining to look over her shoulder for any sign of the cast, she says, 'Good.'

He accepts this because of course his daughter who he thinks is brilliant is ok. It is inconceivable to him that she might be anxious or not-ok and so she does not feel as though she can be these things around him. She wants to be the things he thinks she is. The competent daughter. The on-top-of-things and ever-reliable and always-fine daughter. She is, with him.

'Oh,' he says, patting the front of his jacket. 'This arrived in the mail for you.'

He pulls something out of his pocket and hands it to Lona. A postcard. A glossy picture of Puffing Billy, the old steam train that runs through the Dandenong Ranges. A postcard from Tab. Sure enough, the flipside is covered in spilling, loopy handwriting:

salutations old chum!!

The room erupts in applause as the cast begins to trickle in. Lona struggles to concentrate on Tab's message, and pockets the postcard for later. Martin emerges, waving a cupped hand like the Queen of England. There is still a slight smear of green on his cheek. He sees Lona before she can duck out of sight and he gives her a strange look.

'I came here for Shrek,' she blurts. 'Not you.'

Across the room, Dad is shaking a bewildered Donkey's hand. 'Lona,' he calls, enthused. 'Did you want an autograph?'

Tab's postcard

Lona reads Tab's postcard while Dad's ordering food at the bar. The lighting in the pub is bad and she holds the card close enough to her face that the words stop squirming around.

salutations old chum!!

Tab has always hated capital letters. She thinks they're angular and unlovely. Except for Q's and O's and S's and the obligatory I's. She likes lines that swoop and swish. She likes d's and e's and a's. She likes running them together with m's and n's so that they're hardly legible. She writes like someone whispering loudly. Like she's sitting in the booth opposite Lona and she's just grinned and leaned over to say:

hope this finds you—forgot your new address, woooops!

Em dashes too. Always flat and wide and tucked close to the words at either end. Like a thought that was spring-loaded into the previous sentence. Breathless, like she's bursting to say:

apologies for running off like I did. needed some space & it was one of those now or never kind of things—or like one of those "why not???" kind of things

All the punctuation. Any punctuation, anywhere and everywhere. Wherever it looks nice, wherever it fits. A tiny score of Tab in each tiny decision made, in each bit of blue ink that joins with another bit of blue ink to form a pattern that means something more than scores of ink. Something like:

been to miss marple's for scones & puffing billy (obvs). been walking a lot and thinking a lot. decided to stay a bit longer. hope all is well with you

I can smell someone's wood fire

it's so goddamn pretty up here I want to cry

lots of love,

t

There is no return address. No way of replying. Of writing cheerful words or angry words or sympathetic words or passive-aggressive words. No way of asking: where did you go? In your head, where have you gone? Asking: how long have you been there? I'm sorry, I didn't know. I don't know where I've been.

Dad comes back from the bar still humming 'What's Up, Duloc?' and Lona puts away the postcard. Competent, ok, fine, she reminds herself.

She smiles, says, 'Tab's having a nice time in the hills.'

Sampson messages

Sampson messages something objective like:

Do u want to come to buffy trivia tonite?

Lona receives the message as something subjective like:

I am inviting you specifically because I know you specifically like *Buffy the Vampire Slayer* and I specifically wanted to see you.

He is giving her very little notice, but as a person Lona requires very little notice. She has no plans. She leaves him on read for half an hour and then replies:

Sounds good (SMILING FACE)

Then:

You should know I'm very competitive

He leaves her on read for an excruciating hour and then replies:

I'm counting on it (TROPHY)

It's the sort of thing Lona always used to mistake for flirting. She has finally realised that flirting should not need to be read into. Flirting is not subjective, flirting is objective. Flirting is not when a person knows more than one thing about you and is able to use those two or more things to make conversation with you.

George messages later:

Dinner tonight?

Lona says:

Got plans sorry

She feels slightly bad about it. She considers inviting George along, but George has made it clear how he feels about *Buffy*. He would be trivia dead weight.

They have moved beyond the Father John Misty outburst, but she still feels like she's chafing around the edges where she's started to graze her elbows on the walls of: being with someone. It doesn't help that sometimes the very last thing she wants to do is be close to another person. That some days she doesn't want to talk to anyone, and George doesn't seem to be able to comprehend that he can be part of that anyone while also meaning more to her than almost any of the other anyones.

She knows she should tell him: I'm going out with Sampson. It shouldn't be a big deal. It's her life and she can go where she wants and see who she wants. Sampson's a friend, that's all. She was never going to be: one of those girls. She was never going to let anyone else tell her what to do.

She messages George:

Tomorrow xxxx

One of the boys

They call themselves: Anya Mark, Get Set, Go. They're almost all boys aside from her, which is a buzz, even if they are nerds. There's one other girlfriend—not that Lona is a girlfriend. Lona taps Sampson's arm and says, 'Olvikan.' The others shake their heads, and they write down the wrong answer. They do not realise this is probably the one and only thing in life Lona could not possibly fuck up.

Lona gets a parma like everyone else and enjoys feeling

like one of the boys. Tab would say: this is due to social conditioning to value the respect of men more than the respect of women. But Tab is AWOL so she can't critique how Lona chooses to spend her time.

They do not win. They place in the nebulous unplaced middle with all the other teams who thought they were better than they are.

Lona stays for a beer after, but she doesn't like sitting next to Sampson and not being able to talk to him properly, so she says she has to get home. He says, 'Yeah, I'd better head off too.'

They walk to Windsor station. For Lona it's the same as it always used to be. She enjoys his company. He repeats things that she's said, throwaway things, as if they're funny. She gets the sense that she has the upper hand. The upper hand is unfamiliar to her, but she is enjoying becoming acquainted with it.

'That was fun,' she says, and she means it. 'I like your friends.'

Sampson's friends are easy, or at least they're the kind of people who Lona is easiest with. People who convene to argue about *Peep Show* and *Rick and Morty* before going home to watch *Peep Show* and *Rick and Morty*. With George's friends she feels under pressure to be the optimal version of: George's girlfriend. To be as creative and cynical and intelligent as he tells people she is.

Sampson and Lona both get on the city-bound train. It pulls in at South Yarra and she taps his knee lightly with the back of her knuckles. 'It was good to see you.' She pushes down the part of her that wants to see how far they would go, if ever she were to initiate it. She gets up and steps off the train without looking back.

She blames TV. She blames the unresolved sexual tension between cops in serialised crime shows. She blames anyone who ever insisted that: we're just good friends. Because that must be it. That must be the reason that she can want Sampson, that sometimes she thinks about Sampson and how he would run a thumb along the inside line of her hipbone and how that would feel.

She doesn't want to not be with George. It's just sometimes she also wants to be with someone else. A glimpse of a tattoo on the inside of a stranger's arm can send the blood rushing to her head. She can't help thinking: him, her.

It must be TV, must be something about the fact she never pressed her mouth or her body up against any other mouths and bodies in high school, that she never stopped wanting anyone, everyone, all at once.

Unless it's normal. Unless maybe this is what it's like.

Dog

Ben and Harriet get a dog. They have spent months filling out online breed compatibility tests and after weeks and weeks of Ben getting matched with a shih tzu, he finally managed to rig it so he got what he wanted all along: a dachshund. The puppy is a wriggling thing. It nips at

Lona's toes and the laces of her Docs and it runs around and around until it collapses suddenly, exhausted.

The name of the dog is Edith. Harriet chose it. 'I like it,' Lona tells her. Harriet does not know if Lona is being sarcastic. Lona isn't being sarcastic, it's just that sincerity never leaves her mouth fully intact.

'We were going to get one from the RSPCA,' Ben says, 'but then we found a farm in Kyneton.'

What he's saying is: they wanted a new dog, a fresh one. Not some curmudgeonly old jack russell whose equally curmudgeonly old owner has just gone into a nursing home.

Lona is surprised by how much effort is required just to be in the same room as a puppy. If Edith isn't flinging a rope toy at her, Ben and Harriet are demanding that she acknowledge how much cuter Edith is than any other puppy that has ever existed.

'Have you been in to see Grandpa recently?' she asks Ben, an attempt to short circuit the loop.

He nods. 'Last weekend. They're getting him ready to move into a nursing home.'

'What?' Lona says, surprised. 'He didn't tell me that.'

'He probably didn't want to worry you. You're the favourite, after all.' In his voice, partially buried: sibling rivalry, the most archaic of feuds. Edith drops the rope at his feet and he picks it up and throws it across the room. 'Ahh, look at her!'

Edith runs after the rope and bounds straight back

with it, a boomerang of a dog. She tries Lona, but Lona is distracted. 'I thought he was coming back home,' she says.

'Yeah, he was, but the rehab hasn't gone like they thought. He doesn't have the muscle capability anymore—hey, Hat, get a photo of her like that!'

Harriet already has her phone out and is crouched on the balls of her feet, recording a video of Edith rolling on her back on the carpet. The audio will be an incomprehensible soundtrack of squealing and oh my gaaad-ing. Lona seems to be the only one who remembers she and Ben were having a conversation. Her camomile tea has reached the tepid stage that she loves so that she can gulp it all down quickly. She watches Ben and Harriet tussle with Edith. Sixty years ago, there wouldn't have been a dog. Edith would've been a bun in Harriet's oven.

Lona momentarily forgets what she is doing here. Forgets that Ben is her brother. The same brother who used to find it funny to throw tennis balls under her wheels when she was practising on her skates up and down the driveway. He's a real person now. Lona is a patchwork doll.

She feels slightly ill.

An educative experience

Friday night at Planet Skate, Lona decides to treat the children to an educative experience. She plays them Shed Seven and Hole and The Greatest Band Humanly Possible. They all hate it and beg for the Veronicas, but Lona does it for the one girl who's going to go home and type into Google: destroy my sweater song.

Lona's hair has faded into something closer to grey than blue. The roots are showing through dull blonde. She is wearing old jeans and a big woollen jumper that used to belong to her mother and comes down to her knees. Her heart is not in it, not in anything other than checking her phone every few minutes. It's not like she's texted anyone, not like she's expecting a reply. She hasn't heard from Tab since the postcard.

Pat waves from across the room and shouts, 'Ten minutes!'

Lona brings up a One Direction playlist she has on her iPod for what she maintains is this purpose and this purpose alone. She is forgiven for her previous musical indiscretions. The kids return their skates to the front counter and Lona steps down from her podium and sets about mopping up the place.

'You good to lock up?' Pat asks. 'Tiges are playing the Pies tonight and Bill says it's a close one.'

'Yeah, all good,' Lona says.

She's left the music on shuffle. It's going through her saved songs and playing all the shit ones, or maybe it's just that time of night. Planet Skate feels cavernous with the music and just her. She does the obligatory laps with the hairy mop, collecting all the Fantales wrappers and corn chip crumbs, pushing it all to one side to deal with later. She keeps going without the mop. Her legs feel stiff, but she pushes them regardless, skating so hard into the floor it's like she's trying to crack through. There's a part of her that knows she's doing it on purpose, that the more her body objects, the more she forces it. There's a part of her that's always detested her capacity to be weak, to feel vulnerable. It drives her harder, to hurt more, *feel* more, to legitimise the pain by making it physical.

She can feel the sweat on her back. She turns sharply, skidding so that her legs split and she's reaching out to hold the floor before it holds her. She's ok, just out of breath, her heart racing. She can feel her pulse thrumming in the sides of her face. She gets up slowly and she's kinder then, to the linoleum, to herself. She glides and it is exactly that: gliding.

She turns on her wheels, eyes closed, arms moving through the air around her and finding a blissful nothing in their way. It's sudden, the switch, from frustrated to serene. She's never been able to make it happen when she wants. She forgets, instantly, what it was like to feel anything other than what she's feeling when she's feeling it.

She stops, dizzy, and opens her eyes. Someone is waiting for her, elbows on the edge of the rink. She blinks her smudgey vision, but it doesn't help. There's still someone there.

'Hey,' George calls. 'Don't let me interrupt you.'

It's too late though. Lona skates over to him, feet pushing out in a gentle sideways motion. They stand on either side of the barrier and she begins to roll backwards very slightly without meaning to. 'What are you doing here?' she asks.

'Ouch,' he says, grinning. 'I thought we could get dinner.'

'I'm tired.'

'I don't know if you've heard, but there's this thing called Uber Eats. You press a few buttons on your phone and some poor guy on a bike brings you food.'

He's trying to be funny, but he's not being funny. As girlfriend, Lona feels a certain obligation to laugh. As human being, Lona feels an overwhelming desire to make it stop. She says, 'I've got a bit to do here before I can close up.'

'I can help,' he says. He eyes the clump of dust and lolly wrappers by the edge of the rink. 'I can take out the rubbish.'

'Like a man,' Lona says.

He shrugs. 'Why else would you keep me round?'

She rolls forward so that she can kiss him, lightly, on the lips. It feels like she's giving him something, a gift. She is aware that it shouldn't feel like that. She is unsure why she can't make it stop feeling like one of them is indulging the other. She is unsure how to cede some control without ceding all control, without wanting to take it all back.

'Dust pan is under the counter,' she says. 'Just let me get out of my skates.'

Exam prep

Lona doesn't hear from George for a couple of days, but she only realises it's been a couple of days when he messages:

Sorry it's been hectic this week

Exam prep (UPSIDE-DOWN FACE) (VAMPIRE) (TOP HAT) (BOMB)

I might have to cancel on dinner tomorrow night sorry

She messages:

All good! Good luck!! (RED HEART) (RED HEART) (RED HEART)

It's the first time he's shown any outward concern over his studies. Round mid-sems she'd asked him if he needed to revise instead of watching yet another Noah Baumbach study of bohemian-bourgeois dysfunction. He'd taken her arm in his and turned it this way and that, naming all the bones in her wrist. She called him a smart arse, they watched *The Meyerowitz Stories*. That was that.

The fact he is studying both medicine and music is insane when she actually thinks about it. Especially considering he spends at least three nights a week with her.

He never talks about his theory or clinical units with her, maybe because he thinks she wouldn't understand or be interested. She doesn't know which is worse. She realises, shamefully, that she's never really asked.

They get dinner on Thursday at Fonda on Chapel Street. George is preoccupied. He keeps fidgeting and is doing bizarre things like: not eating his beef brisket tacos the second they are put down in front of him. 'I'm not *worried* exactly, if that makes sense,' he says. 'It's just... I'm worried I'm not worried *enough*, if that makes sense.'

Lona has a gob full of quesadilla, and therefore simply nods.

'I've been distracted,' he says.

'Wha—?' She swallows. 'Getting distinctions instead of HDs?' She's joking, but she can see straight away that she's hit the mark. 'Seriously?'

'It's not good enough unless it's good enough.'

'Says your parents?'

'Says me.'

She shakes her head. 'You're being too hard on yourself.'

'So what? Everyone who's any good at anything is hard on themselves.'

She stares at him, this him she doesn't know. The twitchy, ambitious him. She realises that this is a George he was hiding from her all this time. That she's not the only one who hides things. She wonders why he didn't want her to see this.

She finds his ambition a turn-on. It reminds her of herself. The herself that she misplaced a while back.

'I'm sorry, I think I'm going to have to go into study hibernation these next couple of weeks,' he says.

She says, 'Do what you've got to do.'

In George's absence

In George's absence, Lona finds that it's Tab she misses.

More than before, when she could wedge other feelings, other things, into her days. She misses being talked to, talked about: oh, that's just Lona. She resents her missing, but she misses the pain when she swings at it and only hurts herself. She shuts down, stays in, responds to any invitations she receives: can't go. She gets on with things.

In the meantime, she works a couple of extra shifts at Coles and tramps grudgingly through some Kerouac. Sim gets tired of Lona watching her paint in the evenings and brings home another second-hand easel so they can paint together. Sim paints geometric shapes, and Lona a bowl of pears. Lona has painted before—making it up as she went along in high school, back to basics in the required intro classes at uni—but it was always photography she found most pliable. For the first time, she looks at paint the way she does film. Like it is capable of presenting unreality as likeness. Like it is something alive. She can't remember having enjoyed anything so much in a long time.

George messages at night:

How's your day?

She says:

Good, you?

He sends her an emoticon that her phone doesn't recognise. It shows up as a blank box. Lona amuses herself attempting to guess what he sent her.

A spitting llama.

A whirling dervish.

A solar eclipse.

She doesn't tell him that she can't understand.

Old school stuff

On the morning of George's last exam, Lona sends him a gif of SpongeBob SquarePants giving a thumbs up. She has the day off from work and has promised Mum she will sort through all the old school stuff Mum is attempting to clear out of the study room cabinet.

She catches the train home and helps Mum carry the stacks of art folios and exercise books out into the living room. They stack them on the rug in haphazard piles. Lona notices a year-seven science test sticking out of one pile.

'Jesus,' she says.

'You were the one who wanted to keep it all,' Mum says. 'Something about: I may need this some day. For your memoirs, I assume.' She laughs.

Lona fishes out a short essay written in French she can no longer read aside from the words: Buffy Summers, Planet Skate and Tab Brooks.

'It can go,' she says. 'All of it.'

Mum laughs again, but stops when she realises Lona is being serious. 'Look through it,' she advises. 'There may be something you want in there.'

Mum goes back to the study to work, and Lona clears a space in the middle of the rug for her to sit with her legs crossed. She surveys the task and realises that she couldn't possibly begin without some music. She scrambles across the floor to the stereo cupboard, and finds a few of her old albums jammed in between Dad's various recordings of *Les Misérables* and Mum's New Wave collection.

Barbie Summer Fun Party Volume Two is the soundtrack to her gradual disillusionment. Boy bands and girl groups and 'Strawberry Kisses'. She is ruthless in her culling, bewildered and mortified by her decision to hoard every scrap of validation she ever received in the form of a score out of a hundred.

It's rubbish, mostly. Things she was proud of, mostly. Tests she aced, positive feedback, praise. The occasional C+ she kept in an act of: I'll show them, I'll show them all! Invitations to pool parties, handwritten notes from Tab. Of course it was for the memoirs. Of course it always is. It was important, seemingly imperative, and now it is meaningless. Or, means only: good at school. Whatever that actually means. All she knows is that she would no longer be good at school. Not when it all so clearly means nothing, when it leads only to sitting on her parents' floor embarrassed by the poetry she once wrote from the perspective of Abigail in *The Crucible*.

Lona was undoubtedly a good student.

This is both true and highly irrelevant to anything.

The Saddle Club is singing 'Hello World' when Lona finally gets to her art folios. She had been looking forward to this part, but finds herself turning the pages rapidly, desperately. Maybe doing three forms of art in VCE was what led to Lona believing she could do what she wanted and everything would be all right. She thumbs through her Studio Arts, Visual Communication and Fine Art folios numbly, the pads of her fingers smudging greylead drawings and photographs of Tab with a colander on her head and 3D glasses so that one eye is flashing angry red and the other a cool blue.

'What the fuck?' Lona asks herself.

But all the annotations are full of their own importance and gravitas. Sixteen-year-old Lona believed in herself, but she also believed in the significance of transhuman expressionist art.

The complete loss of faith in herself and her ambition occurs as Lona sits surrounded by all her old school stuff on the rug in the living room of her parents' house. The art that is in these folios is not bad, just as the answers she gave in all those soon-to-be-recycled tests were not wrong.

It's the simple fact that Lona has always done well, but doing well has done nothing for her.

Lona glances around at her work. Almost a decade of being ambitious and good at things. A hundred photographs and drawings and attempts to make something that people look at and call beautiful or weird or whatever she wants them to say.

It's not enough, she realises. It's not enough to respond to a prompt. It's not enough to subvert or to push back on the assessment criteria. Not when she relied on the rubric in the first place, to know what she should be pushing back on, to define the trajectory of her small artistic and conceptual rebellions. Not when she is now so lost without a set of clear directives.

The hollow, pressing feeling in her gut is inevitable, because always, always, always, she returns to the part of her that is tired and scared and tired of being tired and scared.

Because: what's the point?

In any of it.

Lona's phone screen lights up and it's George messaging:

Woooo all done! Do you want to g...

She doesn't click on the message to see the rest because what's the point. She lies down on her back on the floor and she would probably cry if she was the kind of person who cried without instantly challenging the validity of her own emotions.

Mum walks in and says, 'Do you want tea?'

Lona says, 'Please.'

One a.m.

You've reached Tab, or, more accurately, you've reached a digital recording of Tab's voice. Leave a message and I will do my very best not to be such a pernickety smart arse when I call you back.

Beeeeeeeeep.

Sleeping in

George calls in the morning because he is worried that Lona hasn't replied to his messages. She misses the call because she is sleeping in for as long as sleep will have her. When she gets up at 11.30 a.m. she sees the four messages and the missed call and she is irritated that she is required to do something about it.

She is scowling when she sends the message:

Congrats! (FACE BLOWING A KISS) Sorry I was AWOL, phone died yesterday (PILE OF POO)

He instantly shoots back:

Thought something must be wrong

Are you ok?

Do you want to get brunch? (BIRTHDAY CAKE) (COCKTAIL) (GOBLIN)

Lona licks her lips. They are dry and cracked. Probably because she rarely drinks even a single cup of the 32 or however many litres you're meant to drink a day according to Rach. She considers that George wants to celebrate because he is happy exams are over and he gets to, among other things, spend more time with her. She considers that she feels mostly dead inside.

She messages:

I'd love to (SMILING FACE WITH HEART-EYES)

French toast

'Talk to me,' he says. They are sitting in a small cafe in Murrumbeena that appears to have run out of money halfway through construction. Three of the walls have cracks in the plaster through which brick can be seen. There is a bisection of naked pipes beside Lona's head that gurgles every time the toilet is flushed. The cafe won Best New Eatery on some website somewhere and it is packed.

Lona cuts another too-big-for-her-mouth piece off her French toast. She smiles. 'What do you mean? I'm fine.'

He groans. 'You're not fine. Can't you understand how frustrating it is for me when there's clearly something wrong but you don't want to talk about it?'

She says, 'This French toast is delicious.'

'Lona!'

'There's nothing wrong, George,' she snaps. 'This is me. This is all me. This is me this morning. I'm eating French toast and I am *fine*.'

Lona looks at her breakfast so that she doesn't have to look at him. All she wants right now is to be at home watching the musical episode of *Buffy*, but telling George that would only lead to ridicule, or worse, a sigh. He is the reason she is here instead of there and so she can't help being annoyed with him.

'Tell me about the exam,' she says, using the classic diversion tactic of pretending to be interested in his thing.

'I already did,' he says.

She obviously wasn't listening and she is obviously being a shit girlfriend. She says, 'Oh, sorry,' and pushes a dollop of mascarpone onto her forkful. The food is so good but her mood is so bad. The taste and her disposition are cancelling each other out until all she feels is numb and slightly queasy because she is eating so fast.

George rubs his forehead like he's got a hangover.

His hair is hanging in lank strands over his face. She remembers him saying thát he was distracted, that being distracted was a problem. That it was bringing him and his GPA down.

Lona is the distraction. Lona is the pounding, unrelenting ache in his forehead. Lona, or the frustration of being with Lona when Lona is so unpredictable in her wanting to be with him.

George takes off his glasses so he can knead his eyes.

Hypothesis

They climb up the temporary scaffolded staircase to get to the new Murrumbeena sky rail. The station, with its sterile concrete aesthetic, is clearly worth the $1.6 billion dollars the government threw at it. The next city-bound train is in twelve minutes.

'We're in two different relationships,' George says. 'You're in a relationship with me and I'm in one with you, but they're not the same.'

It's obvious to Lona that this hypothesis is too slick to be something he just came up with. Which means he's been thinking it for a while. 'But couldn't that be said of all relationships?' she asks. 'I mean, technically, isn't subjectivity always a thing?'

He groans, exasperated. 'See, there! You're responding to the wrong part.'

She blinks a couple of times and wonders if they are fighting. She has never fought with someone close to her before. She is scrambling for data with which to interpret this conversation. Unfortunately, her only data comes from teen TV shows from the '90s. 'So, what? You're breaking up with me?'

'What?' he says, stunned.

Potentially *Heartbreak High* is not the place to turn for advice. But Lona can't stop now. 'Well, you want me to change and I don't want to change. So that's that.'

George looks hurt. 'I don't want you to change.'

'You don't want to want me to change,' she corrects. 'But you don't want me to be like this and I am like this.'

He reaches for her hand. 'You're being stubborn.'

'Yes,' she says. 'I am stubborn.'

The park down the road

Lona starts to go for walks, late in the afternoon when the park down the road is a roiling pack of dogs and dog-people. She does laps while her head does laps. In the almost dark, she circles closer and closer to the centre of the oval until she is simply turning on the spot.

At home, she finishes painting her pears and she sits the canvas on top of her bookshelf so that she can stare at it until she switches off her lamp at night. It is so beautiful, and Lona is so proud and surprised to have made something so beautiful.

George messages and Lona replies, belatedly.

Later sometime, spiralling ever closer to the middle of the park oval, she asks herself over and over again: what are you thinking, what are you thinking. She says the words out loud and they block out any possible thinking.

She is exhausted with someone being in her bed, her phone, her reasons for doing things. She is exhausted by sharing. She sits down in the centre of the football field and feels the back of her jeans go instantly damp with dew.

'What are you thinking?' she asks.

The break-up
The break-up is so effortless it's almost indecent. There is not enough of them materially in each other's lives to make it cumbersome. There is only a hoodie returned, a book. There is only incomprehension, the feeling of entering a house after being outside in the sun, of blinking until their eyesight adjusts. There are photographs on film not yet developed. There are words and songs that will remind them of one another, strings of messages that will be pushed further and further down the inbox as time goes by.

Lona finds that she misses him. She finds that it aches. But what doesn't?

Movie night
Rach brings up categories on Netflix and clicks through to Romantic movies. Lona says, 'How about Action?' She wants to watch something with Jason Statham pulling off a heist using only a crowbar and his thick cockney accent.

The smell of fatty acids is permeating the house. There are potato gems in the oven. There are peanut M&Ms in a bowl. If Lona was at home, Mum would have bought wedges and sour cream and a block of Top Deck chocolate. Sim and Rach don't know her so well. They are guessing because Lona never tells them anything about herself.

Rach does not want to watch Jason Statham pull off a heist using only a crowbar and his thick cockney accent, and like always, she wins. She does strike a compromise though. *Shaun of the Dead*. The girl's got ok taste, Lona will concede that.

'I'm really attracted to the guy from *Black Books* in this,' Sim says. 'Like, I don't know why. He's such a tool. I think I'm attracted to tools. Problem is, they're tools.'

She is perched on the arm of the couch. Sim always perches on the arm of the couch. Lona always says, 'There's room on the couch.' Sim always says, 'I'm ok. I'm not going to watch the whole thing.' But she inevitably does, from the arm.

'I'm really attracted to Simon Pegg,' Rach says. 'But not like in this. Like, now. Like, 40-year-old Simon Pegg.' She twists her hair back into a bun and tucks it into itself so that it stays done up, even without a band. Rach's hair is big and thick enough for it to work. Lona has tried to do it herself. She gets a little knob that unfurls as soon as she lets go. Lona hasn't washed her hair in two weeks. She has decided she's never going to wash her hair again. Shampoo is a consumerist construct, like razors for women. The internet says so. Tab once sent her a link.

Lona hasn't received a message from anyone in five days.

Sim opens a bottle of pink moscato. They drink it from mugs. It's been months, but still the only crockery they own is mugs. Sim gets out her sketchbook and does scenes from the movie. Rach rubs the pendant at her neck, the Sagittarius archer. The timer goes off for the gems and thankfully it's Sim who gets up.

'Not too much salt,' Rach calls.

Lona can hear the prolonged crunch of the grinder. Sim brings the gems out crunchy and sodium snowflaked. She squeezes Lona's shoulder. Lona understands that this is all being done for her. Sim and Rach only just found out about the break-up, even though it happened a week ago. They are doing these things to make Lona feel better. They are avoiding asking any direct questions and Lona is glad.

She doesn't want to talk to Sim and Rach. She barely knows Sim and Rach, not in any of the ways that really count. She wants to talk to her parents, or Tab. Not about George. About books or films or the correct use of the word *literally*. She doesn't want to be here, in this home that isn't a home, with these friends who aren't friends. She wants to be alone. She wants to be able to watch a movie and laugh at all the bits she wants to, not the bits she feels she can around other people.

She wants George.

Stupid, true, not all the time.

He said: relationships are about always being there.

But always is obliterating. Always is asphyxiating. Lona has never been able to stay still inside the arm of another person.

She takes a potato gem hot off the plate and it scalds the inside of her mouth.

She watches the movie and she laughs when the others do.

Tab gets back

Tab gets back from Sassafras and apparently turns her phone back on. She messages:

heard about george

i'm sorry

u ok?

Lona can feel the sediment of hurt and resentment stirring in her stomach, but she knows it would be hypocritical to begrudge her friend for wanting some time alone. She replies:

I'm all right. How was your trip? Do you want to get lunch sometime this week?

The green dot indicating Tab's chat window is active disappears after a minute. Lona waits for it to reappear. It doesn't. She is on her break. Muesli bar in fist on the back step by the dumpsters. She closes her chat window. Opens it again.

Still nothing.

Selfie

'Ahh, you're doing a selfie,' Sim remarks, coming to stand behind Lona. Lona cannot paint when there is someone standing behind her. She does not want to look like she cannot paint when there is someone standing behind her. She makes a couple of insubstantial strokes on the canvas, blending blue into blue.

Lona is painting her first ever portrait. She is, of course, painting herself. Lona used to joke in high school: I am my own muse. Sometimes it was the more self-effacing: I am the most available subject I have. Or: if I'm going to digitally manipulate someone's face, I feel most comfortable using my own. She could never say it like: I like looking at pictures of myself. Even though that is the truth.

She is painting her face front on, staring at herself. It's not her, not really. Her skin is yellow blue pink. Her hair is silver blue white. She uses a thumb to smudge a bit of Paynes Grey beneath her eye.

Sim cocks her head. 'It's a bit choppy,' she says.

Lona doesn't know what she means, but she also knows exactly what she means. The colours are all there, they're just not cohesive. She steps back and looks at it.

The left eye is wrong and she doesn't know how to fix it. The lips are too full.

'You know when everything is shit...' she says.

Sim claps a hand on her shoulder. 'Keep at it, Loney.'

Tab replies

Tab replies so late that Lona forgets what she's responding to:

> bit busy at mo with uni
>
> soon ok

Lona is unsure how to proceed when she knows more about Tab's situation with uni than Tab realises. Lona hates that she knows. She hates that she isn't better at being there for her friend. She hates that she spends more time thinking about how inconvenient it is for herself. She messages:

> All good (SMILING FACE WITH SMILING EYES) How is everything going?

Tab replies:

> same old

Lona types out a couple of responses. One so earnest she backspaces immediately, afraid she is going to unintentionally send it and then the truth will be there forever in a blue speech bubble and it will sit as a line of code in a machine in the desert and someone will find it one day and use it against her and that's how she'll be remembered.

Her panic and frustration curdles fast into apathy and in the end she leaves it. Doesn't say anything. The not saying anything is so relieving, so anarchic, it buoys her. So Tab needs space. That's fine. Lona pockets her phone and goes back to painting.

The car ride there

Sampson has a housewarming for the house in Preston he has moved into with his brother and his brother's friends. Lona doesn't know anyone else who's going. No one else from uni has clicked attending on the event.

She has borrowed Mum's car and she listens to '90s punk on the way there, turned up loud with the windows down. The lead singer was most definitely on crystal meth when it was recorded. It just zings right along.

She's wearing jeans and a black turtleneck. Lipstick that is too orange for her face. Her hair is mangy. It's been almost a month since she last washed it and it is pulled back into a low, greasy bun. She is trying just enough to make it seem effortless. She is having conversations with Sampson, glancing at the empty passenger seat as if he is there. I'm glad I came tonight too, she tells him. She imagines it's darker than it is.

Where are we going? no one asks.

Just wait, she says.

She takes a wrong turn and the GPS on her phone starts to shout at her. Next left. Next left. Next left. Her phone is jammed into the cup holder. She can't see the map. When she takes her eyes off the road for a minute she almost hits the car in front of her.

Shit.

The Sampson in the passenger seat is gone. It's just the music and her singing along: I could crush you like a bug/ I shouldn't have said that. The line peels over into the next one so it half-rhymes. Lona likes that. There's something satisfying about the way it sounds.

She parks two houses down because the street is crammed with cars. She sits in Mum's car for ten minutes thinking that she couldn't possibly go in. It has taken her 45 minutes to get here. She is frozen still. If she leaves now then no one will ever know she was here. No one will miss her.

She misses Tab, because this is always when she needs her most. Tab as human shield. To duck behind in a room full of people. To belong to, beside. But Tab is not here. Tab has not been here for some time.

In her place, a hope niggles at Lona, selfish, horrible: maybe for once she can be the one that people like.

She checks her makeup in the mirror. She gets out of the car.

Inside the house

She finds Sampson in the lounge. 'Lona!' he says. 'You made it!' She gives him his gift: a toilet brush. 'Um, thanks,' he says.

'Four boys sharing a house,' she says. 'I can only imagine the carnage.'

He looks at her and smiles the way he does with only one side of his mouth. She is fairly certain she is going to kiss him tonight. She is fairly certain he's thinking the same thing. He hugs her. She has missed it, the press of a body on her own. She thinks of George. She doesn't want to think of George.

'Where's the food?' she says. She hasn't eaten since lunch. Parties make her nervous and she can never eat before them.

'We've only got chips,' he says. 'We'll probably get some pizza later. Do you want a drink?' He asks the question in this way that makes it clear he's saying: I want you to have a drink. So they're both in that slightly sticky space where things happen. Good things.

'I'm driving,' she says. 'But maybe half a can.'

'The esky's in the kitchen. You can help yourself.'

She doesn't want to leave him because she knows that she can't come straight back to him. That this is his party. That he belongs to everyone tonight. That she's going to have to do a round of the room first. But her mouth is dry, her lipstick feels scaly around the edges of her lips. 'All right,' she says, and edges through to the kitchen.

There are a lot of people. She doesn't see anyone she recognises, not from uni, and not from trivia. The esky is on the floor beneath the sink. She tugs out a Somersby and turns around and there's a girl there. 'I love your hair,' the girl says.

'Thank you,' Lona says.

The girl is also wearing a turtleneck and jeans. She has dark hair pulled back into a high ponytail. She has a necklace with a fox on it.

'I like your necklace,' Lona says, because girl law

dictates a counter-compliment must be proffered in such circumstances. Genuine admiration is not a relevant factor. Scan opposing body for notable clothing and/or hairstyle. Employ flattery.

The girl waves a hand in an instantly familiar: oh you! 'It was my mum's from like aaages ago,' she says. The deflection of compliment: equally critical enactment of girl law.

Lona pulls the tab on her cider and realises this girl has her cornered. She looks exactly like the kind of girl Sampson would have been friends with at school. A bit nerdy, a bit odd. A bit like Lona.

'I don't know anyone here,' Lona says.

The girl says, 'I'm Melanie. Now you know one person.' Even though Lona cannot recall anything funny having been said, Melanie laughs so hard she snorts. Her lipstick is cranberry red and magnificent. 'How do you know Sampson?' she asks.

'Uni,' Lona says.

'Ohhhh, of course. Groovy girl like you. Of couuurse you're from design. Do you know what you're going to do after?'

'It was Fine Arts actually,' Lona says. Then, 'I'm already after.'

'You've graduated?' Melanie asks.

Lona looks over Melanie's shoulder but there's no sign of Sampson. 'I dropped out and now I work at a supermarket,' she says. 'I get up in the morning because someone pays me to get up in the morning. Being alive to see the next season of *Stranger Things* is just about the only thing that keeps me going. So did you go to school with Sampson?'

Melanie blinks. 'I...no, I'm his girlfriend.' She laughs a little bit, this time without a snort. 'I've never seen *Stranger Things*,' she says. 'But I've heard it's good.'

Lona stares. Tries to comprehend that the girl she is staring at is not just a girl friend but a girlfriend. The two words shoved together in a formation that means one very specific thing: Sampson is fucking someone else, and the same someone else repeatedly. 'It's the greatest TV show since *Buffy*,' Lona says. 'Please excuse me.'

Drunk

There is a can of cider in her hand. The can is cold, wet with condensation. Her hand is wet with the wet. She wipes her palm on her jeans whenever she meets anyone, holds her hand out to shake. It's still clammy and cool when they take it.

Everyone is just a bit afraid of her, the way people are when there's a girl speaking loudly to people she doesn't know and nodding along like she understands their high school in-jokes. She is drunk and seeing in technicolour. She can't remember why she's hurting, so everything chafes a bit.

There is a can of cider in her hand—but it must be another one. It's cold, straight out of the esky. She does not remember being inside the esky. She talks to Sampson's brother Reagan who she keeps calling Rogan Josh. Behind her in the lounge, Sampson has his arms around Melanie.

'Rogan Josh,' she says. 'I'm meant to be driving home but I think that I probably shouldn't do that now. You and Sampson have the same ears, did you know that?'

'That's all good, you can crash,' Reagan says, then he turns around to someone he actually wants to speak to.

Sampson's room

Lona likes being in people's rooms when they're not there. Sampson's room. Boy room. Chaotic and boy-smelling. George's room was so neat. Cello in the corner. Bass on a stand. Bookshelves with their perpendicular lines. Sampson's books are piled up all over each other. Most of them aren't books, they're magazines or graphic novels. Graphic novels are books. The Bechdel test. Taste is just another name for internalised misogyny.

Lona remembers she lent Sampson a book last year. He hasn't given it back. She didn't like it but she thought he would like it. That was a bad sign. She thought it was crappily written but that he would think it was good. Taste is just another name for thinking you're better than everyone else.

'Lona?'

Sampson is in his room, which makes it instantly and infinitely less interesting than when he was not in his room.

'Give me back my book,' she says.

'What?' he says. He steps towards her and his hair is longer and his girlfriend is taller than Lona but only just and they have the same turtleneck and the same intention of getting in his pants.

'The book I lent you,' she says. 'Police special task force. Ghouls. Werewolves. Dry sense of humour. I want it back.'

'I haven't finished it yet.'

'I want it back,' Lona says, trying to smile. Because it's a joke, it's all a joke. Ha ha. She attempts to seductively lean back against his bookshelf, but her shoulder hits with more force than intended. The whole thing shudders. Sampson holds out a hand that almost comes into contact with her arm. It just hovers there.

'You're such a nerd, Specs,' she says. They're close. Lona can feel it, there between them. She's not imagining it. It's there.

'Here,' he says, and he's holding something in front of her face. 'Whatever, Lona.' He leaves her and she turns the thing over in her hands. The book she leant him. There's still a bookmark in it, about a third of the way through. Shit, he's a slow reader. She could never really be with a slow reader.

'Sampson,' she calls dully.

She sits down on the edge of his bed. Her head is sloshing. Eyesight furry around the edges. She lies back and she tells him: I'm here, I'm where you want me. She rolls onto her side, pulls her knees close to her chest. She's never been this drunk before. Empty stomach. Nervous before parties. Sleep now.

This isn't her bed.

It's a big bed, big enough for two, three, four. Top to tail like the grandparents in *Charlie and the Chocolate Factory*. Top to tail. The music's loud. 'Roald Dahl was a terrible person in real life,' she says. It smells like him. Sampson. George. Someone closes the door because: there's a girl passed out in there.

The morning

The morning is a rank taste in her mouth. No one closed the curtains so the light burns the backs of her eyelids until they are crisp. She opens her eyes and she doesn't remember and the not remembering is terrifying. She pats herself down, but she's fully clothed. There is no one else in Sampson's room or Sampson's bed. Only her.

She gets up and she knows she's going to vomit. It's been a long time since she last threw up, but her body knows what's happening. The bathroom is across the hall. She hugs the toilet bowl and it gulps out of her. Just liquid, bile.

She wipes her mouth with toilet paper and then sits on the toilet, pisses into her spew. Hello, hangover.

There are voices from the other room. Lona does not want to see Sampson, or anyone. She wants to crawl out the window, but this bathroom doesn't have a window. She curses Sampson and his windowless bathroom. She curses herself.

She was stupid and stupidity is dangerous when you're a girl. The world doesn't let girls be stupid. If they're stupid then whatever happens to them is their own fault.

Her head dips unintentionally, her body calling her down for more sleep. She spots the toilet brush she gave Sampson, now taunting her from beside the bowl. 'Shut up,' she tells it. She laughs, despite herself.

She washes her hands and splashes water on her face. She used waterproof lipstick last night. She has to scrub her lips raw to get the last of it off. Her hair is so greasy she wants to cry. Shampoo might be a consumerist construct, but without it she feels hardly human.

There's a knock on the door. A tentative, 'Lona?'

She says, 'Yeah, you can come in.'

Sampson opens the door slowly like he doesn't quite believe her. Their eyes meet in the mirror. 'I'm sorry,' she says.

He shrugs. 'It's ok. I just slept on the couch.'

She nods, wants to ask about Melanie, wants never to ask about Melanie, wants salty scrambled eggs on thick buttered toast. 'Apologies, I almost had to christen the toilet brush,' she says.

Sampson grimaces. 'Reagan already did last night. You were right, Lona. Carnage.'

She turns around to face him. 'I don't think I can drive yet.'

He nods. 'You can stay as long as you want.'

Long shower

When she gets home, Lona has a long, long shower. She washes her hair and then conditions it until it falls through her fingers. She finally agrees with Belinda Carlisle vis-à-vis heaven's locality on earth.

Independence

Grandpa has been shipped to a nursing home called Independence or Autonomy or something similarly preposterous for a facility that operates for the sole purpose of housing the un-independent. Mum rings to let Lona know the address.

'I think you should see him as soon as you can,' Mum says, then seems to realise how ominous that sounds. She hastens to add, 'He's been missing you.'

Lona gets a train and then walks the rest of the way. She cannot get into the nursing home because there is a locked door and keypad and she doesn't know the code. She rings Mum again but Mum is apparently otherwise occupied. She presses her face against the glass sliding door and ogles the woman on the front desk until the woman gets up and opens the door from the inside.

Lona explains that she didn't know the passcode and the woman explains that the passcode is necessary as residents are often doing pesky things like expecting to be allowed to leave the nursing home.

Lona has scrawled a room number on the back of her left hand, but she can no longer tell if it's 18 or 73.

Thankfully no one here is trusted to remember their own name or room, so each door is marked with a piece of cardboard. The piece of cardboard is slotted into a metal clamp and can be easily slid in and out like the patients in the rooms. The door to Grandpa's room is closed. Lona knocks.

'No tea,' he shouts from inside.

'It's just me, Grandpa,' Lona says, opening the door.

He's by the window in his wheelchair. He's had his hair cut, but not in the way he likes with the short back and sides. It has just been sheared down all over. He has been looking out the window into a courtyard with three white plastic chairs and a wooden trellis table. He smiles when he sees it's her.

'Lona.'

She glances around the room: the unmade bed with sheets so thin she can see the waterproof mat through them, the box of tissues, the jug of water, the bedpan on the floor. She does not know where Grandpa's things are. She doesn't remember what Grandpa's things are.

'Hi, Grandpa,' she says.

He shucks his wheels back and forth until he is facing her. He is wearing elastic-waisted shorts and his catheter bag is strapped to his right leg. It is half-full.

'How's it going?' she asks.

'Good, good,' he says briskly. 'How are you?'

She picks at the skin around her thumbnail. She doesn't even realise she's doing it. The skin there is peeled back and raw. 'Yeah, good, good.' She looks around for somewhere to sit. There is an armchair cradling a stack of plastic bags and tubes. There are metal rails on either side of the bed. She puts her bag on the floor and continues to stand. Her body doesn't like standing. One side of her always eventually starts to sink. Her left leg bends so that her hip moves out of alignment and then she is lopsided. She is comfortable lopsided because she has been conditioned to be comfortable lopsided.

Lopsided = unobtrusive = non-threatening

Like most girls, Lona has made an art form of making herself seem smaller than she is. It is difficult to fight this urge when it has been hereditarily gifted.

There's another knock on the door and Grandpa bellows, 'No tea!'

A carer enters the room with a plastic tray in plastic gloved hands. He puts it down on Grandpa's table. 'No tea!' Grandpa repeats. The carer leaves and there's a plastic cup on the plastic plate beside a plastic-wrapped biscuit and the cup is full of tea.

They both stare at the tea.

'I need to get out of here,' Grandpa says.

Lona fishes out the book she's reading. It's early, but she's desperate. She pushes the bags and tubes back and sits on the edge of the armchair. 'The narrator is an AI,' she explains, before she begins.

'A what?' Grandpa asks.

'An artificial intelligence,' she says.

'A what?'

It's a science fiction novel about a mammoth spaceship that has been sent halfway across the universe to colonise a new planet. There are dangerous space molecules and laser guns and problems with the ship. There are always problems with the ship. The narrator is the artificial intelligence embedded in the ship that starts to question the meaning of life. Grandpa starts to question the meaning of the story.

'Can the robot feel empathy?' he asks.

Lona blinks. 'No. But it can conceptualise it. Also, it's not a robot.'

'Why would a robot think in human language?'

'Because it's programmed to...I guess. I mean, I don't know...but it's not a robot robot, like I said...'

'*1984*—now *that's* a good science fiction novel.'

There's another knock on the door. A different carer comes in for the tray. 'Oh, you didn't want your tea,' she says.

Lona sees the fury flash behind Grandpa's eyes, but it's gone, withered, in a split second. Because the carer is gone and the tray is gone, without waiting for a response. 'Five bloody times a day,' Grandpa grumbles. 'Tepid and weak as anything. I'd murder a man for a decent cup of tea.'

Lona remembers the kitchenette she passed on the way in. She could offer to make Grandpa a cup of tea the way he likes it. Milk, no sugar. But that would mean staying and she doesn't know if she wants to. She doesn't know if she's a properly shit person or just an ordinary person.

'I think I'm going to take a nap,' Grandpa says.

He stares at the wall until she goes.

Stack

Lona has her earphones in listening to Dolly Parton. She is working nine to five at Coles today, and has been listening to the applicable song on repeat for approximately an hour. It's cold and her fingers are numb and blue except for on the tips where they are bright red. She links up a stack of trolleys with a lime green strap and pulls tight.

Her gloves are almost worn through across the palms. Her vest is inside out and no one has told her. Her hair is nearly faded back to the bleach.

She has, against all odds, started to enjoy her work. She likes that she doesn't have to talk to anyone. She likes that she can feel the muscle in her arms and it's because she's actually doing something, not just going to the gym. She likes that she now wears the same t-shirt every day to work and no one cares.

She pulls the trolleys out of the bay and swings them around. The sound of the wheels on the asphalt is thunderous, drowning out Dolly and Lona as she breathlessly sings along. It's after three and the car park is chockers with mums and kids. Lona can smell the end of the shift.

One of her earphones falls out of her ear and she

reaches for it, a one-handed grip on the trolleys as she rounds a corner. She's missing the last chorus, which is the best chorus. Her cold fingers struggle to plug the earphone back in. The weight of the trolleys tugs on her arm and she clamps both hands on the handle a moment before a kid steps out in front of the stack.

'Shit, watch out!' she yells, jerking the trolleys away with all she's got.

The little boy looks up and stands there, frozen, as the trolleys skid past him. Lona's hold breaks, and they go barrelling away from her. 'Fuuuck,' she says, running after them. A car backs out of a space up ahead and Lona knows what's going to happen and of course it does. There's the thunder of the wheels and the squealing grind of the stack making contact as it collides with the rear of the SUV.

She's got her hands on the bar and she's pulling the stack back and there's another scream as it scrapes across the bumper of the next car along. She pulls it tight, gets it to stop, but the damage is done.

The woman in the SUV is out and saying things. The mother with the kid is pointing fingers. Lona is standing in the middle of the car park with her hands locked around the bar and the commotion has shaken up her iPod Nano making it auto-shuffle and now she's listening to 'Welcome to the Black Parade'.

The trolley at the front is crusted with red and silver paint.

Fuck.

The manager

The manager, the big manager, the manager of all the other managers at Huntingdale Coles, offers Lona a chocolate croissant from an open carton. '$2.99 for a packet of six,' he says proudly.

There is a picture of the manager on the wall of his office. In the picture he is surrounded by the members of Status Quo and their Down Down Prices Are Down guitars. The manager is smiling in the picture.

The manager is not smiling at Lona.

Her hot pink iPod Nano is on the desk between them, as is her vest.

'I'll get my stuff out of my locker,' she says, through a mouthful of puff pastry.

'I'm sorry, Kim,' the manager says.

'My name's not Kim,' she says. 'It's Lona.'

Fired

Old Kim is outraged that Lona has been fired. 'I'll quit if they don't reinstate you,' she vows, but Lona knows that she can't afford to. She knows that Old Kim will be here for a long time, longer than Lona ever would have been.

Old Kim gives her a hug and it is fierce and Lona is secretly devastated. Tony is openly devastated. He is now returning to trolleys. He does not know how this is going to impact on his relationship with Yasmin from the express checkout. He is too angry to say goodbye to Lona. Kel slips her a twiggy stick. Everyone else has already forgotten who she is.

Lona peels off her gloves and chucks them into the bin on her way out. She catches the train to Carnegie. She doesn't know what she's going to do now.

She watches TV.

Meme

Lona doesn't tell anyone that she lost her job at the supermarket. Sim and Rach must notice she's around the house more often, but they don't say anything. No one ever says anything to Lona. It's like they're scared to. There's this assumption that she knows what she's doing and that no one should question it. She really wants someone to question it. So she can yell at them and tell them they're wrong.

She finds herself thumbing her phone absentmindedly, and she knows it's Tab she wants to speak to. More than that, it's Tab she wants to hear from. Not just the occasional message or tagged meme about *The Lizzie Maguire Movie*. She doesn't want their friendship to dissolve into a meme-tagging friendship. But she doesn't know what to say. Doesn't know how to say: I'm aching and I don't know why. Doesn't know how to deal with an honest answer to the question: how are you feeling. So she doesn't say, doesn't ask. So she sees a funny meme about Struggling At Uni on Facebook and she types the @ symbol and then Tabitha Miranda Brooks, the whole name because Tab's never been afraid of giving all of herself. She doesn't ask: are you struggling at uni?

Tab usually replies with a comment:

lols

ahahaha

but like 100% accurate

Lona misses her hyena laugh.

Death on the Nile

Lona borrows one of Grandpa's copies of *Death on the Nile*. She's at home for dinner and she sneaks into Grandpa's room. Ben's room. Whoever's room it is. She stands staring at the bookshelf and then she takes one. She takes it back to her place and puts it on the coffee table in front of the TV and thinks about reading it.

Mostly she watches TV. When she gets sick of watching TV she just sits. She picks up *Death on the Nile*, but it's nothing to her. It's one of those days, weeks, months.

There's a tube of black paint stuffed between the couch cushions. Lona finds the tube in her hand and she uncaps it, presses the mouth to the centre of the pages she's struggling to read and squeezes, leaves a big gloop that seeps into the spine. She stares for a moment, indifferent to this thing she has done to this object that isn't hers.

The paint is black black against the yellowed pages. She presses the book shut and holds it between her hands like a prayer. She doesn't know what she is doing. She is doing and the doing is exciting.

She opens the book to the same pages, has to peel them apart from one another. The paint has spread and bloomed across pages six and seven like a Rorschach test. She sees a skull in it, a horse, a wildflower. It looks sticky and wet like an oil slick, like automotive grease. She presses a thumb into it and smears a line so it's no longer symmetrical. She blows on the paint, wills it to dry, so she can turn the page over and start on a new one.

Frank

She is making. It's nothing yet, or nothing complete yet. Her mood is titanium white and her paint is black. It's a series of experiments more than anything. It's a what if. It's a can I. She paints the title page with a large flat dry brush so that it's like a hairy spirit surrounding the text. She paints the edges of the paper and finds this seals the book shut. She has to peel each page away from the others with a satisfying tear.

She blanks out words with a swipe of a deliciously stinky permanent marker. She circles others, random words:

the
smile
water
her

that mean nothing and are suddenly significant. She pulls a scalpel out of her pencil case and carves out phrases. She paints the cover. She gives it a new title: postmodern d'art. Inside she writes over and over again the same thing: are we post-postmodern or are we just insane? Art school theory chirps in the back of her head: deconstructionism, baroque, modernity, Warhol, Duchamp, ceci n'est pas une pipe. She cuts up squares of Fred Basset cartoons and lines of Leunig poems and sticks them in with masking tape. She tears out pages and sticks them back upside down. She is making.

This thing, at times it is so horrendous to her that she abhors it. She calls it Frank, short for Frankenstein. 'Alas! Life is obstinate, and clings closest where it is most hated,' she recites for no one, making her wonder why her sixteen-year-old self felt the need to commit that to memory. She tosses Frank across the room and then goes and picks it up again.

She is making.

Dinner party

Nick hosts a dinner at his place for Tab's birthday. Lona receives her invitation via Nick. This is a hundred forms of hurtful. But when she gets there, dressed in a multi-panelled leather jacket she refers to as her Technicolour Dreamcoat, she realises that this is not Tab's party. Or at least: it is not a Tab party.

Fleetwood Mac is on the stereo, but Lona knows Tab likes Taylor Swift and the Pussycat Dolls at parties. The wine is red, to go with the ragu. Lona digs out the cider she was hustling in inside her handbag.

Tab appears, dressed in the exact same skirt and shirt combination she wore last birthday. She squeezes Lona's hand, which she has never done before. It's like it is a wake.

There's just a handful of them, and although this is for Tab, Lona's never met half the guests before. Lona watches the door, wondering if George will arrive, not wanting to ask if he's coming for fear of it seeming to mean something.

Lona watches Tab across the table and realises she doesn't have anything to say to anyone here except for her friend. Tab pontificates, gestures, laughs, knocks over a glass of wine in her enthusiasm to pass the butter.

Lona reaches into her pocket and squeezes the tiny parcel in there. Tab's present: a set of earrings shaped like hairy legs. A little card attached with red ribbon, the card little so she didn't have to worry about coming up with something profound to say. Just: happy birthday bud. The person next to Lona is talking to her.

Tab looks over and smiles.

The back step

They sit out on the back step together. Tab says, 'I'm flunking out of uni. They're not going to let me continue Arts. Mum's spazzing out.'

Lona says, 'Oh shit, I'm sorry.' She is relieved she no longer has to feel bad about not bringing it up.

Tab pulls her long hair back and ties it with the red ribbon. The hairy legs are dangling from her earlobes, flashing pink painted toenails. 'I had to go to a review with the head of the faculty.'

'What are you going to do?' Lona asks.

Tab shrugs. 'I'm thinking of being a train driver.'

Lona stares at her. 'What?'

'Well, why not?'

'Well, why?'

'Why anything?'

They can't remember what the original question was or anything they're talking about. Lona gets this scary feeling that she hardly knows her best friend anymore and she wonders if she's falling out with Tab without realising it. But that can't be it. If anything, it feels like they're hardly moving.

'I got fired,' Lona says.

'Shit. What happened?' Tab asks.

Lona shrugs tiredly. 'I don't know. I used to be good at things.'

'You can be a train driver with me,' Tab offers.

'I honestly can't tell if you're joking.'

'Neither can I.' She cackles, and then sighs. 'I'm going to break up with Nick.' She says it like a premonition, like an oracle, like there's no way she can stop it.

Lona doesn't know what to say. She feels suddenly, unexpectedly sorry for him and his not-knowing.

'He's so nice to me, Lone, and I'm so nice to him.' She leans backs against the railing, eyes half shut. 'I'm unhappy and I need to get my shit together.'

Nick's lounge room

Tab goes to the loo and Lona wanders back inside. The party's dead, just Nick sitting in one chair and George in the other. Lona feels the cascading progression from surprise to elation to panic. Her nose prickles with the smell of pot. George has the joint pegged lazily between his knuckles. 'Hi,' he says.

'Hi,' she says.

The longing is a swarm of wasps: painful, buzzing. His gaze on her is like peroxide. She can feel the surface of her skin begin to peel.

She glances at Nick, wonders if he knows that Tab's thinking of ending things. She wonders if Tab will even go through with it. Tab says these things. She makes pronouncements, pledges, vows. Cuts her metaphorical hand with the metaphorical blade and swears *Outlander* is the greatest TV show she's ever seen. Everything is absolute until it suddenly isn't. Until she stops watching *Outlander* three episodes into the first season. Lona never knows how seriously she should take her, even about the serious stuff.

'Tab's tired,' she tells him. 'She was heading to bed.'

George passes Nick the joint and Nick takes a slow, savouring drag before handing it back. 'Yeah, cool. I'll see how she's doing.'

He gets up and leaves them alone. George is staring at the blank television. He is just this side of: pleasantly baked. Lona is unfortunately just this side of: feeling the alcohol whatsoever. She waves a hand at the armchair Nick vacated. 'You mind?'

He shrugs.

Lona sits, crossing her legs at the ankle like a proper lady. She checks her phone and thumbs at the screen like she's dealing with something important, not just opening and closing Shazam repeatedly. George says, 'I thought you must've left.'

She nods. 'I was about to head off.'

He looks at his watch. 'Shit, it's only 10.15. This party sucks.' He grins at her and even though he's cooked and that's probably the only reason he's being nice to her, it makes her insides swim with affection.

'I'm sorry, George,' she says. 'I'd never done it before, so I didn't know how to do it so it didn't hurt.' She frowns, hearing the words back. 'To be clear, I'm talking about breaking up, not sex.'

He laughs groggily. 'Lona, it always hurts. But yeah, you did a shit job.' He takes a small nip at the burning nub. 'To be clear, I'm talking about sex, not breaking up.'

She rolls her eyes, approximately 82 per cent sure he's joking. 'Jerk.'

Nick comes back into the room, barefoot, carrying a black electrical cord that he tosses at George. 'Try that. I used to use it with my MIDI keyboard, but I think the connection is the same.'

George looks at the plug. 'Hm, yeah. Thanks.'

'Bad news is, we're hitting the sack, so...' Nick glances

between Lona and George, says, 'What's that song? Closing time, time for you to leave...' He not only butchers the lyrics, but also the melody, in a voice that Lona finds satisfyingly lacking. 'Unless you want to crash,' he offers. 'Which is a-ok.'

'Nah, I'm going to head home,' Lona says, standing.

She half-expects George to get up beside her and declare: me too. She half-expects them to slip backwards into being with each other. Half-expects him to get into the Uber with her, to wait until they're standing on her front porch to kiss her. To stand there groping each other so long that the sensor light goes out and then it's just them in the dark until she says, 'You want to come in?' And then there would be the being with him. She half-expects it to be like that, easy like there was never anything in between.

But he says, 'I might crash if that's all right.'

Lona orders an Uber and Tab appears in her Golden Snitch pyjamas with her hair in Pippi Longstocking plaits like she's worn to bed since she was seven. She pulls a face when she sees George. 'You good?' she whispers to Lona.

Lona nods but she is secretly devastated because she half-expected that George would beg her to take him back and she half-wanted to agonise over taking him back. Nick pulls the bed out of the folding couch and George goes to the bathroom and Lona's Uber arrives and Tab walks her to the front gate in her ugg boots, all the while Lona looking back over her shoulder.

'You can't have it both ways, Lone,' she says.

Lona says, 'Neither can you.'

Tab hugs her and Lona hugs her back.

The worst advice

Sim turns Frank over in her hands and then passes it to Rach. 'It's cool,' she says. Rach leafs through the pages, running a finger over the twisted masking tape and the paint spills. 'Very...cool,' Sim repeats.

'It's shit, isn't it?' Lona says, dismayed, hope deflating, the indifference as scalding as a blistering critique.

'No, it's not shit,' Sim says quickly. 'It's just...what *is* it?'

Rach turns the book upside down and says, 'Ooh, Fred Basset!'

Lona slumps down onto the couch. 'I don't know what it is. I don't know what it's for. I just made it and it's pointless and stupid. Do you think I would make a good train driver?'

Sim takes the book back from Rach and flicks through it. 'No,' she says. 'I think you should make more of these.'

'You said it was *cool*,' Lona argues.

'Cool is a good thing.'

Lona shakes her head. 'Cool is what I say when I can't think of anything nice to say.'

'That's because you're a shit person,' Sim says. 'I say cool, I mean cool.' She hands the book back to Lona. 'Just do what you want to do.'

Lona groans and leans her head back into the couch. 'That's the worst advice I've ever received.'

A spattering of banter

It starts with something like a throwaway:

the matrix s on 11

SWITCH ON UR TV NOW

She messages:

Way ahead of you Specs (SMIRKING FACE) Do you think I could pull off a full-length leather jacket?

It's a spattering of banter throughout the film about Hugo Weaving's sunglasses that turns into something like a conversation, or whatever passes for conversation when people interact through the tapping of thumbs.

They've been going on-and-off for four days when Sampson messages:

going to a bar tonite thats got games n pinball

dont know if ur interested

Sampson types fast at the expense of grammar and punctuation. She hopes this is also the reason he spells like she used to on RaNdom Gurrrl, the blog she made when she was ten years old.

Lona looks at the invitation and gets a squirmy gut feeling that's the usual swill bucket of anxiety and anticipation.

She knows that Sampson has a girlfriend. She knows that and she would never *do anything*. Not unless he did first. She's not the kind of person who'd get between people. Not unless he made it clear he and Melanie were done. Which he won't and so she won't, and therefore the verdict is: it's fine.

It's all morally and emotionally fine.

She replies:

I'm interested.

Commodore 64

The bar is in Collingwood, which is further north than she'd usually trek, and she spends the entire train and then number 86 tram ride telling herself it's not just because of Sampson.

She reminds herself that she has never been in love with Sampson, and that love is just a strong like, and she finds it difficult to strongly like anyone for an extended period of time.

The bar is called Commodore 64. It is essentially an arcade for people who can legally consume alcohol. There are screens and hoop machines. There are chess boards and a giant Jenga set and blink-182 on the sound system. Lona finds Sampson down the back hunched over a *Lord of the Rings: The Twin Towers* pinball machine with half a dozen other sweaty, excited young men. She recognises a couple from the *Buffy* trivia night. One she doesn't remember says, 'You're the girl who passed out at Sampson's.'

Sampson gives his friend a shove. 'Lona, you're here.'

Melanie is not here. This feels significant, but it is

probably not. Lona makes sure her hopes are kept at a base minimum. Keeping her hopes at a base minimum has sustained Lona for many a year now and she's not about to change tack.

'You want a drink?' Sampson asks. One of the others produces a jug of beer and a grotty glass she is 99 per cent certain was just swiped off a nearby table.

'I might check out the bar,' she says.

Butterbeer

Sampson buys her a Butterbeer, and a couple of drinks down the track she buys him a Malteser Falcon. 'It's like a milkshake with burning in it,' he says. They play chess while they're still sober enough, and then clamber in and out of whatever arcade machines are free.

She drags Sampson into the photo booth. 'First one, nice one. Second, stupid. Third, freestyle,' she instructs. When it spits the photos out it's just three indistinguishable frames of them cacking themselves.

It's sweltering inside the bar and after a bit Lona needs water. She sits by herself on a padded bench seat, waiting for an attractive nerd to spot her and decide that she is: the perfect girl. Sampson joins her after a bit, sitting close enough she can feel the heat radiating off him. He's got sweat at his temples. Lona wants him so much it hurts.

'Where's Melanie?' she finds herself asking.

Sampson frowns and his cheeks get hot. 'Home.'

'Why isn't she here?'

215

'Lona.'

She realises she has hit a nerve. She wonders if she feels vindicated, or even happy. Mostly, she feels the Butterbeer. 'Come on,' she says. 'I want to play Dance Dance Revolution.'

Every Thursday night

Going to Commodore 64 is apparently something Sampson and his friends do every Thursday night. Lona soon finds herself among the people who are weekly called, messaged or a barrage of both, until she confirms that she's coming. She doesn't stay out as long as the others, because she's the only one who lives south of the river. The train ride home is always an adventure she is too tired to enjoy. She Ubers home from the station, or walks if the night is clear enough and the vibe pleasant enough that she isn't afraid she's about to be blamed in tomorrow's paper for her own murder.

What she finds is that she enjoys being with Sampson, because it is easy. It feels good to be friendly and all the things that being a friend entails: the smiles and nudges and stories. She thinks: this is enough. And it is, mostly. She misses the closeness she had with George, but the thought of being that close to Sampson, to anyone else, still nauseates her.

She gets to know Sampson's friends and their degrees and their favourite television shows. She develops feelings for approximately 55 per cent of them.

When they start calling her Ramona Flowers, she is so happy she could die. Tab would say: the manic pixie dream girl is a male fantasy. But it feels so good to wear black chokers and pink tights and tight denim shorts and have boys look at her. It feels so good to believe the things they believe about her.

She can be her over-analytical, self-defeating self anytime. She's not going to waste an opportunity to be someone else.

Smith Street

Sampson follows her out of the bar, stumbling slightly on the step. She pretends she hasn't seen and he pretends he doesn't know she's pretending.

'Argh, I can't be bothered getting home,' she complains.

'Stay at mine,' he says.

This should never have been said and both of them are aware of this and so it is no big deal. She just says, 'Argh, I hate that you make me come all the way over here.'

She's thinking she's just going to Uber home. She has the app up and she can see all the drivers in their black cars whirling around in her hand.

She catches the toe of her boot on the pavement and trips slightly. Sampson catches her arm and this time they both pretend that they can't feel the hot of each other's skin.

'Four minutes until Arjun arrives,' Lona announces, looking at her phone. Sampson's just standing there now,

217

at her side. He's blushing, or drunk. Lona looks at him and his hair and his face and his daggy t-shirt and she finds herself saying, 'I like you, Sampson. As in I'm into you. You know that. I mean, you know that, right?'

He blinks and says nothing, which is probably the appropriate reaction. He finally says, 'Oh.' Arjun is pulling around the corner. Sampson's eyes are going from side to side like he's doing some sort of equation in his head and then he ducks his head slightly and Lona wonders what he's doing and she realises he's about to kiss her and she steps back.

He stares at her. 'Oh,' he says again.

There is too much drink, too much blood, too much night in her head. Sampson is pulling at his shirtsleeves and avoiding her eye and she doesn't know what she wants. She remembers: this is what you want.

She reaches and gets his jaw and she kisses him. Lona mouth on Sampson mouth. They're still too-warm and clammy from the bar. A couple of nerds making out on the footpath, and he's not very good at it, or she's not very good at it, but then no, that's just how it is at the beginning. Just the way it is when you're working out how to be with someone else, how to get inside someone else.

She can feel the want between her legs and she pulls away for a second and there he is, Sampson, and for a moment she's horrified about the fact she's got Sampson's spit in her mouth. And she realises: this is not what you want.

Lona's phone buzzes. It's Arjun calling, wanting to

know where she is. He is idling at the kerb. She is idling at the kerb. There's a part of Lona that wants to go with Sampson, even as she's realising a whole lot of her doesn't.

'Lona,' he says.

She doesn't know how to tell him the truth. That she wants to fuck everyone she ever meets. That she doesn't want to fuck anyone.

'Goodnight,' she says, and gets in the car.

Next week

Sampson doesn't call or message. Thursday swings around again and there's no invitation to Commodore 64. She's glad and hurt.

She finds herself wanting him again, the way she always does. It's easy when he's not there, when no one is.

It's just feelings though. Effervescent, unremarkable feelings. It's just feeling lonely.

The following Thursday she gets a message:

u in fr the commie?

Commie being slang for the most un-political bar that ever existed. Lona stares at the message and thinks she's probably going to fuck it up eventually, but if that philosophy stopped her from doing things, she would have a thoroughly Emily Dickinsonesque existence.

She goes and they don't speak about it and it's weird, but it's not the worst.

'I'll see you next week?' Sampson says at the end of the night.

She says, 'Yeah, why not.'

Youth Saver

Lona hasn't checked her bank account in a couple of weeks. She has been applying the if I can't see you, you can't see me rule to her balance. Rach hands Lona a post-it note like she always does when it's that time of month.

One post-it note for Sim and one for Lona. One ball-busting number on each. 'Gas has gone up,' Rach tells them. Lona looks at her post-it note. An amount of money she doubts she can cover and a smiley face. She brings up the dreaded Youth Saver account on her phone. She has $758.43. It is enough to cover this month's rent, but that's about it.

Lona transfers Rach the money and a fist of anxiety grasps the back of her throat. She knows there's only one thing she can do.

Out in the lounge, Sim and Rach are having dinner. Lona hovers at the edge of the room divider, watches them. These girls she has so very little in common with. Rach with her horoscopes and her granola. Sim with her MDMA stashed in her sock drawer.

'Hey,' Lona says. 'I've got some bad news.'

Moving back out

Dad drives around with the station wagon and helps Lona load all her things into the back. Rach makes him goji berry tea and sits with him while he drinks it. She laughs at every second thing he says. Lona has the distinct feeling that Rach is angling to be her new mummy. She says, 'Dad, we've got the bed left and that's it.'

'Lucky you didn't buy a new one,' he remarks.

Lona looks at her bed, sitting stripped at the end of the room. It can fit on the roof of the wagon, which is a plus. It can fit almost anywhere.

Rach and Sim have a new girl moving in next week. It feels like the end of an era. Everything feels like the end of an era.

There are hugs and nice things said.

In the car on the way home, they listen to the *Beaches: Original Soundtrack Recording* that has been stuck in Dad's car stereo for almost three years. He says, 'It'll be good to have you home.'

Hipster cafe

Ben gets a promotion at work and wants to take the family out for lunch. He chooses a hipster cafe in Bentleigh. Lona orders hot chips and they come out under a glass dome. The waiter lifts it away with a flourish and sets the wooden board down. There was smoke inside the dome and it curls up into the ceiling. The chips taste like she's sticking her mouth into the ash of a bonfire. The world is, undeniably, insane.

Harriet says, 'To Ben!'

They clink water glasses and empty coffee cups. Ben passes his phone around the table saying, 'Look how much Edith has grown!'

Mum and Dad are very proud of their son. They nod at each other when they think no one else is looking, thinking: job well done. Ben helps himself to Lona's chips and grimaces. 'Ugh, god, that's disgusting.' Lona watches him go back to eating his smashed avocado on vegemite toast and says nothing.

'Sorry to hear about Coles, Lona,' Harriet says.

Lona says, 'Thanks Hat.'

Power saver mode

Mum and Lona visit Grandpa at the nursing home. Grandpa is in a bad mood. He doesn't want to talk about anything other than the things that the nurses are doing wrong. He is convinced there is some conspiracy to do with his television screen. 'They keep switching it off when I'm watching it,' he says.

Lona spends most of the visit going through the television settings. This way she can do something and not feel so useless. This way she can not feel so bad about not wanting to talk to him. She works out that the power saver mode is active. She switches it off. 'It should be ok now,' she tells him.

Grandpa is not out of bed. He hasn't been out of bed in two days. The physio is too much. 'When was the last time you had a shower, Dad?' Mum asks.

'Did I tell you about that nurse, the Indian one, trying to give me the wrong pills?'

Mum smiles tightly. 'Yes, Dad, last weekend.'

He purses his lips and doesn't say anything more. Mum asks Lona to get Grandpa's electric shaver charger out of the drawer. Lona notices that the polaroids, one of her, one of Mum, have been knocked down behind the chest. She picks them up and puts them flat on the bench top. She hands Mum the charger and Mum plugs the shaver in. 'Do you need us to do anything else?' Mum asks, and Lona can hear the desperation in it. The desperation for the answer to be no.

Grandpa says, 'It's fine, fine.'

Lona thumbs the polaroid of herself with her blue blue hair. It was taken over a year ago now. In the other, Mum is smiling, hair tied back, the strap of an apron around her neck. Both photographs are slightly bent. Lona's about to tuck them in her pocket for safekeeping but Grandpa looks across at what she's doing. 'My girls,' he says gruffly, protectively.

She puts them back.

A bath

Lona stands at the door to Ben's old bedroom. It is void of Ben. Void of Grandpa. The single bed, a twin of Lona's own, is made up. Ben's bed has never moved from this spot, never shifted beyond an inch or two, and even then it would leave marks in the carpet that showed how long it had been in the one place.

The books on the shelf are sagging sideways without

bookends. Ben's Alex Rider and Grandpa's P.D. James. Lona pulls an old book out. The title has rubbed off the spine. She opens it to the title page: *The Underwater-Man.* The paper is thick and creamy. She presses her nose into it and breathes deeply.

In the next room she runs a bath. She has to rinse it out first because no one's used it for yonks and it has collected an unappealing drift of fingernail clippings and stray pubic hairs. There's no bath bubbles in the cupboard, but she finds a stinky Lush bomb she remembers getting for something like her seventh birthday. She chucks it in and it hits the bottom of the tub with a clunk and roils and fizzes.

She gets out of her clothes before the water's ready so she sits on the cool edge of the bath and her nipples go hard and wrinkly and the hair stands up on her legs and she's fatter than she was two years ago and has hair in places no one ever told her she was going to get hair, but she's tired of fighting the way her body wants to be.

She gets into the bath and tucks her hair up behind her head and starts on Grandpa's book. It's boring. She drops it into the water and it sinks. She pulls it out, dripping, and stares at it. Dunks it under again, for good measure. Lets it sit in the bottom of the tub with the bomb grit and the Lona grit while the water gets cool and her skin gets pruney.

She gets out and pulls the plug. The water runs out with the suck until it's just the book sitting there in the sandy basin. She should hang it on the clotheshorse or fritz it with the hair dryer until the pages bloat and buckle. Stop it from going mouldy.

She should.

She goes into the kitchen and gets a takeaway container from last night's Thai. Puts the sopping book inside and seals it shut. Because: what's the worst that can happen. Because: what are you afraid of.

Zine launch

Lona photographs a poetry zine launch at Pink Triangle, an installation event space in Fitzroy. There's not a big turnout. There are a couple of readings and a man in the corner playing house music through his laptop speakers. Lona finds herself talking to the owner of the space.

'How much would it cost to rent this place for the night?' she asks.

Rudi is a short woman with a platinum blonde crew cut. She flicks her eyes up and down Lona. 'How about you shoot my daughter's bat mitzvah and we'll call it square?'

'Oh, I wasn't actually thinking...' Lona squeezes the shutter release. The camera's off and it doesn't do anything. Just ping ping pings. 'All right,' she says. 'Sounds fair.'

An ok outcome

She messages a few people and a few people say no. Sim and Rowena, Lona's old softball bench buddy, say yes.

'If it's lame and no one shows up, then we can just get

drunk,' she tells them. They all agree that this is an ok outcome.

Sim is going to show her paintings of lines and triangles. Rowena is going to exhibit a bioform feminist sculpture she's been working on. 'It'll literally make you sick,' she assures Lona.

Lona continues to raid Grandpa's books, building up a Frankensteined collection. It feels less like destroying than recycling. She decides there's no point in having books in the end, not if they can't be read. Mum questions whether this might similarly apply to Lona's own books. Lona chooses to cite artistic prerogative.

At night she can't sleep because her mind is buzzing. She has become used to the anxiety that burrows into her chest at night, and it takes her a while to realise: she's not scared, she's excited.

George's face

George's face shows up on Lona's Facebook feed. It's a surprise really. Usually they're the same. Trawlers, not posters. Thumbing through other people's photos, videos, in-jokes. Feeling a little bit a part of it without being involved.

But here he is, a grainy picture taken in the band room at the Worker's Club. His hair is scuffed up a bit at the front. His mouth is curled halfway through saying something like: put that thing down. It's posted by Hello Hello, the band's page. The caption is:

get down here before the g-man is too fried to play (WINKING FACE) doors open 8. we're on from 10 (OGRE) (GOBLIN) (TRUMPET) (GUITAR)

Lona closes her Facebook tab. She feels uncomfortable, irritated, frustrated. It occurs to her: she wants to go.

The Worker's Club

She can hear 'About a Girl' through the walls. It's thrumming with strings and a rat-a-tat kind of percussion that takes a while to get used to. Lona hands over ten dollars to get to the person she wants to see.

They're a jumble on stage. More people than instruments almost. George is there, left side of the stage, fingers going plug plug plug on the frets. He smiles at the rhythm guitarist. Lona can't remember his name. Josh or John. She's invisible along the wall, back pressed against the naked wooden beams.

The next song is an original. Lona remembers some of the words:

this night this night your eyes your eyes

George gets right up against his microphone to sing the harmony. It's lyrically challenged. It goes round and round in circles talking about a girl like she's everything anyone could ever want. Lona is pissed off by it.

She scooches to the bar. Orders a vodka, lemon, lime and bitters. Elbows pressed in on both sides by other jean-clad sleeves. Everyone's wearing at least two items of denim. She feels like she's in a cult.

'Lona?'

Lona looks back and blinks at the face attached to the neck attached to the arm attached to the hand that's on her shoulder. 'Nick,' she says. 'Hi.' She glances around automatically.

He says, 'She's not here.'

Lona doesn't ask, can't think of anything more uncomfortable than asking. Tab could simply be at her place, too tired to come out. If the breaking up hasn't happened, if he doesn't know, Lona doesn't want to be the one to pull that decidedly un-magic rabbit out of a hat.

'Does he know you're here?' Nick asks, getting way too close to her in the process. She can feel his saliva in her ear and the tickle of his beard.

She shakes her head.

The beer garden

Nick seems to be by himself, or at least: he's making himself by himself. He and Lona sit in the beer garden. She says, 'I'm still on the fence about Murakami. And show me one woman who likes *The Trial*.'

'I could show you twenty.' He squints at her. 'You always think you're right.'

The band spills out after they've packed up the set. They're loud and laugh a lot. Gigs transport them back to the people they were in year eight music class, playing together for the very first time.

She looks up and George is there, receiving a clap on

the back from someone she doesn't recognise. They offer him a cigarette and he declines. He's got his fist around a half-consumed pint of something dark and fermented. He glances up and sees her and she watches the way what he was saying falls right off his lips, pulling the corners of his mouth down in the process.

She looks back at Nick. 'When do things get less weird?'

He shrugs. 'Sometimes they don't.'

George takes an absolute age to get to them, even though he must know it's inevitable, even though he keeps looking over when he thinks she's not looking. When he finally arrives he stands at Nick's shoulder, bumps him with his now-empty glass.

'What's up?'

Nick shrugs.

'Hello,' Lona says, too softly.

'Hello,' George says, too loudly. He looks away. 'Your hair.'

'Yeah,' she says. It's dark with semi-permanent dye. The girl at Hairhouse Warehouse assured her it's going to fade back to something like her natural colour soon enough. Back to the wistful, wasted blonde she's never done anything with, that she's never used to: have more fun.

George has never seen her natural hair. She wants him to see it. For this not to be the last time. She wants to know him for more than one hairstyle.

He sits. 'What's been happening?'

'I'm doing an art show next week.'

'Cool.' He doesn't ask about it, which makes her slightly disappointed and slightly annoyed, both emotions she realises she is not entitled to anymore considering his and her no longer being together and his consequent right to find anything and everything she says or does deeply uninteresting. He says, 'Have you been watching *Game of Thrones*?'

Which is ok. Which is better than nothing. She rolls her eyes dramatically. 'Don't even talk to me about it.'

'I know right.'

Nick is on his phone and Lona tries to care about him, but finds she can't and if she's a shit person, well, she's a shit person. She looks at George across the table and thinks: that's my friend. She feels the warm and the: I should be so lucky. She feels the love love love. It opens up inside of her and the beer garden is full of it, full of people, and sometimes, occasionally, she likes people.

'So how are you doing?' he asks.

She nods, smiles. 'Yeah, all right.'

Art crap

Lona is fossicking through her art crap. Her art crap is the collection of brushes, beads, pencils, stamps, stickers, blades, sketchbooks, needles, Copic markers, inks, paints, paper scraps, embossing plates, scissors, calligraphy pens etc. etc. that fill three out of the five drawers in her dresser.

She has started working on her fourth book. It's a

tiny hardback edition of *Mansfield Park* from the 1930s. It's probably worth something. Lona is about to make it entirely worthless with the assistance of whatever sequins and coloured feathers she can unjam from the corners of her top drawer.

The top drawer won't open properly. It's jamming on something in the next drawer down. She opens the second drawer and reaches in, holds it flat so she can pull the obstruction out. It's her Van Gogh chain-smoking skeleton tote bag, lumpy and full of something.

Full of undeveloped film.

She shakes the canisters out onto the floor and they tumble against one another. It's been ages since she took a photo she wasn't paid to take. She opens the bottom drawer. She's got a half-empty bottle of fixer. 'Hm,' she hms.

Negatives

Lona turns the second bathroom into a darkroom. She tapes cardboard over the window and nicks a draft snake from Mum and Dad's room. She pours the developer into the first canister and seals the lid. Gives it a good shake.

She's never done prints like this before, but she's consulted Lord Google. God bless the interweb. She tips the developer into an ice-cream container and fills the canister with fixer. Lets it sit. Watches her watch.

She rinses the negatives and then goes out into the other room so that she can have a look. It's a roll from June last year. A couple of shots of Grandpa and Mum. Then a whole bunch she took at Pujita's farewell. She squints at the cell in which Nick appears for the first time. The next one with the three of them.

She spends the afternoon developing film. Some of the rolls are from two years ago. There's another one in which George pops up in every second frame.

Five rolls in she comes across a series of shots she doesn't remember taking. Pictures of a beach she doesn't recognise and a backyard she realises is Grandpa's. It doesn't look right though, the trees are different. There's one of Lona in a tree. Lona squints at it. She doesn't remember climbing a tree—in fact, she's certain she hasn't climbed a tree since she was in primary school.

There are more of Lona. Her brow creases. Who took them? She brings the film so close to her face she's seeing more of the kitchen through it than the actual photographs. It's not her, she realises. None of them are her. The woman looks like her, but she's older. She's got a different mouth.

She remembers: the film canister that was in the Pentax when Grandpa gave it to her. The roll of film that'd been in there for at least two decades.

These are photographs that Grandpa took.

'Grandma,' Lona says aloud, staring at the woman she never met. She's only ever seen her in her wedding photo, the one Mum keeps on the mantle in the lounge. The wedding photo was taken at a strange angle, the Grandma in the wedding photo doesn't look like the woman in these pictures, doesn't look like Lona.

There she is, sitting in a tree. Hand shading her eyes. Smiling at Grandpa.

Lona goes up the other end of the house and knocks on the door of the study. 'Mum,' she says. 'Come look at this.'

Haircut

Tab shows up unannounced. Mum and Dad are in Castlemaine for their wedding anniversary and Lona has been working on her books. *The Underwater-Man* is looking pretty festy. She's cut a cavity in the pages of *Children of Men* and is attempting to construct embryonic fluid out of glitter glue and Clag.

Lona answers the door with scissors in her hand and Tab looks at them and says, 'Perfect, I want a haircut.'

Lona thinks that Tab is joking, but Tab is not joking. She explains to Lona that her hair has never given her joy and Marie Kondo says that if something doesn't bring you joy then you need to thank it and get it out of your life. Lona has no idea what Tab is talking about. She points out that she has never cut hair before. In fact, the scissors she is carrying are pattern-edged blades.

Tab says, 'Even perfecter.'

She drags a kitchen chair onto the back lawn. 'Lob it off like a ponytail,' she instructs. 'Someone can make a wig out of it.'

Tab sits down and pulls her hair over one shoulder and grabs a fist full of it in her hand and brings it close. 'Thank you,' she whispers, and then kisses it lightly. There's a moment when she just holds it, like she's frozen, then she blinks and tosses it back so it hangs down the back of the chair. Desert red and bum long. Not for long.

'Are you sure?' Lona asks. She's always wanted to cut someone's hair. She's not going to ask twice.

'One hundred per cent,' Tab says.

Lona gathers Tab's hair into a bunch. It's so much thicker than Lona's hair. There's so much of it and it's so much of Tab. Lona opens the scissors and makes a cut. It doesn't do anything. The pattern-edged blades are not sharp and certain enough.

Lona squeezes the scissors open and shut. She saws and hacks.

Tab is shaking. Lona is so preoccupied with the task at hand that it takes her longer than it should to realise her friend is crying. Or something in the region of crying. Laugh-crying. Sputters of it.

'Are you ok?' Lona asks, hesitating.

'No—shit,' Tab says, leaping up. 'This is crazy, what am I doing?'

Her hands go instantly to her hair and her whole body relaxes when she finds big fistfuls of it. She clutches at it like the intrinsic part of her conception of self that she never wanted it to be. She turns to Lona and her eyes are blurry around the edges. 'Lucky you didn't...'

She stops and stares at the small bouquet of hair Lona is holding in her left fist.

'Shit,' she says.

Lona is attempting to freeze her face in something like solemnity, but she can't help herself. The laughter is like projectile vomit, everywhere all at once, and she's bent over hacking it up.

'Shit,' Tab says again. She finds the short bunch of hair at the back of her head and she holds onto it. Her mouth is wobbling with the effort of keeping it straight. 'It's not funny,' she says.

'Not at all,' Lona can barely say.

Tab's mouth tears at the seams and they are both laughing then, louder and louder the more their eyes meet. Tab takes the hair from Lona and holds it in her cupped please sir I want some more hands, like it's a baby wombat or a ball of blown glass. 'My darlings,' she gasps hysterically. 'My poor, poor darlings.'

Lona blinks the saltwater from her eyes and she can feel it dash down her cheeks in fast, warm streams and the backs of her knuckles are there catching it and reabsorbing it into her skin.

'I'm sorry,' she says, and Tab says, 'What for?'

Lona grins. 'I have an idea.'

An ordinary type burial

It's an ordinary type burial. A hole is dug and the dead are laid in their grave. Lona has picked a spot down by the back fence where several goldfish have turned to toothpick bones. 'Farewell, my dearests,' Tab says, and licks a few biscuit bits off her Golden Gaytime.

Lona takes a bite out of her own ice cream and uses a plastic beach spade to refill the hole. 'They died beholden to nothing and nobody,' she says. 'They were the bravest locks of hair I ever knew.'

Tab crouches and uses her free hand to pat the earth down. A couple of stray hairs poke up through the dirt defiantly, refusing their deathbed. 'We were so good together,' she sniffs.

They finish their ice creams and then Lona uses a twist tie to bind the sticks together into a cross. Tab plants it into the garden bed.

They stand in silence for a minute, looking down at the roughly assembled grave.

'This was weird,' Tab says. She slings an arm around Lona and fits her head into the Tab-shaped crook of Lona's neck. 'Thank you.'

Exhibition

Lona gets to Pink Triangle early, plastic ziploc bags full of mutilated books under her arm. Rudi unlocks the door for her and says: 'You make a mess, you clean it up. Noise off at eleven or the neighbours will be on my arse. Capiche?'

'Capiche,' says Lona.

She drags a couple of plinths out from the back room and sets her books up. Covers closed, two to a plinth. She puts a box of rubber gloves next to *The Underwater-Man*, in case anyone's keen for a fondle.

She pulls a couple of bottles of seven dollar white wine out of a biodegradable shopping bag and puts them on the foldout table. Puts the hummus and crackers and Black & Gold cheese next to them. Bon appétit.

Before she forgets, she pins the print she made of Grandpa's photograph onto the back wall. Grandma in the tree, grinning. Lona grins back.

Rowena shows up, panting, at the window. She signs something through the glass, but Lona has no idea what she's on about. Lona opens the door. 'What's that?'

'Had to park fucking miles away,' Rowena wheezes. 'Couldn't drag it myself. Need help.'

They carry the sculpture between them. It's a giant papier-mâché piñata. It is strangely heavy. It smells. They set it down in the centre of the installation.

'The Monopoly Man?'

'It's an ode,' Rowena says.

'It's a $10,000 HECS debt,' Lona says.

They both grin.

Sim's late, which is no real surprise. Other people show up before she does, and they start milling around. Rowena's art school friends pose with the Monopoly Man, who is now swinging dangerously from the ceiling. Others paw through Lona's books. There's not much else to do, so they stand around and talk. Lona plugs in her hot pink iPod and brings up something boring and trendy.

Tab sweeps in with her usual aplomb, wearing a long floral dress that doesn't quite reach her Grandad Shoes.

Her hair is braided several times and in several directions around her head so that there is no way of telling a chunk of it is missing. She makes a beeline straight for Lona with her hands held out in front of her. Lona feels the grin crawl across her already flushed face, because it's her friend, Tab, and she feels giddy, relieved, excited, always, every time she sees her crossing the room to get to her. Here she comes.

Apologies and excuses

Lona's phone shimmies in her pocket with apologies and excuses. The whole gamut of reasons why people aren't coming:

a) father's birthday
b) boyfriend's football club presentation night
c) intense cramps
d) streaming *Doctor Who* same time as the UK

She turns her phone to silent, and then off. Doesn't even read the one from Sampson. Doesn't even check to see if George has replied to the message she sent yesterday. Tab gets them both wine, served in a *Frozen* plastic cup with Olaf the snowman melting on one side and smiling on the other. Tab stands at Lona's elbow and Lona stands at Tab's elbow and sometimes they go talk to other people.

Sim bursts in with two canvases under each arm. 'Argh, there's no hooks!' she exclaims. Lona points out that there are indeed hooks, in fact multiple hooks, but Sim says,

'There's no time!' She takes the foldout chairs out from under several people and sits the paintings on them.

Rach trails in after her and tells Lona, 'The new girl snores.'

A song that was big five years ago comes on and people start to sing along. Lona looks over her shoulder and sees Tab dancing with a person Lona is 95 per cent sure Tab just met. The grin sits in the corner of Lona's mouth and refuses to budge.

She turns back to Rach and nods while Rach talks about burpees.

The main event

'All right, now for the main event!' Rowena announces, clapping her hands together as she clambers up onto a chair.

Despite being the organiser of this exhibition, Lona was not aware that there was a main event. Someone pauses the music despite Lona's hand-scrawled note promising: touch the music and die.

Rowena lovingly pats the side of the Monopoly Man's bloated face. 'It's time to demolish this fucker!' she shouts. Lona belatedly notices that Rowena is holding a baseball bat.

Tab leans close. 'I don't know what's happening, but I love it.'

Rowena jumps down from the chair, violet Docs smacking the floor. She gets into a good position: feet shoulder-width apart, two-handed hold on the bat. She wriggles her shoulders a bit, making a show of it like she always used to back in inter-school sport. The other girls on the team used to hate it, but this room is loving it.

'Step back! Step back!' Rowena swings and the bat smacks into the Monopoly Man, sending him careening away and then straight back into another swing. Rowena turns and offers Lona the bat. 'Left field?'

Lona takes it. The room is hot and full and loud and Lona is a sponge, soaking it all up. She mimics Rowena, getting a good grip on the bat and then smacks it into the piñata. There's a cheer. Lona hands the bat along.

Lona notices that her parents have arrived. They're standing just inside the door wearing nice clothes. 'You came,' she says.

'What on earth is going on?' Mum asks.

Lona glances at the door and then the photograph of Grandma on the back wall. 'Where's Grandpa?'

'He wasn't feeling up to it. He's sorry.'

There's a sudden gasp and cacophony as the piñata bursts. Whooping and stamping and then a smell hits the room. Someone groans. 'Oh, Jesus, *what*?'

Lona turns in time to see a cascade of pellets pouring from the wound in the Monopoly Man's belly. Mum crinkles her nose. 'Is that...'

There are tampons waterfalling onto the painted white floor. The tampons are soaked with what Lona hopes is brown paint.

Needless to say, everyone realises they've very suddenly and inescapably got other places to be.

Wet wipes

Rowena is on the floor with a ten-pack of wet wipes. Sim and Rach are sitting drinking what's left of the wine, while Tab and Lona box step to Ace of Base. Mum and Dad are up the street at a restaurant that doesn't smell like menstrual blood. Lona will join them eventually.

Tab grabs Lona's hands and they wash the dishes dry the dishes turn the dishes over. Sim and Rach get up and join in. 'What about that one that went like oranges and lemons something something lemons?' Sim asks.

'Ring the bells of St Clements,' Rowena says from the floor.

'Or ring-a-ring-a-rosy,' Tab suggests.

It's just after nine. An earlier night than was anticipated, but then the night has so far been many things that weren't anticipated. Lona finds herself held on both sides by hands that swing her round and round. She can see Grandpa's photo every time she goes past. Grandma in the arms of a tree. Lona in the arms of a tree.

'Ugh, I feel sick,' she says, stumbling away from the others. Her head is giddy black dots and she slumps on a foldout chair, laughing.

Photo frame

Lona puts a cup of tea on the wheeled bench and moves

it closer to Grandpa. It's still steaming. Dash of milk, no sugar. Just made, by Lona, in the kitchenette. She slips off her backpack and unzips it. 'I've got something for you,' she says.

Grandpa is in his wheelchair, but he's not speaking. He gazes out the window of his room into the bare courtyard with its plastic chairs that always seem to be fallen on their sides. She takes out a bundle. She's wrapped her cardigan around a photo frame. She takes the frame out and shows it to him.

He glances at it. For a minute Lona is afraid he isn't going to respond. Then he takes it from her. The picture of Grandma in the tree.

'Where did you get this?' he asks. His voice is croaky and sick sounding.

'The Pentax,' she explains. 'The roll of film that was in there.'

'I took this?' he says.

'Yeah,' she says. She tries to imagine not being able to remember taking a photo. She's not lived long enough to know what it's like to forget.

His hands are shaking. The doctors still don't know what's wrong with his legs. Multiple sclerosis. Parkinson's. Lyme disease. They've given up because in the end he's old and so: what does he expect. Something will go wrong and so: at least he's got his mind.

This place is bad for him. It's made him not-him. Lona can see that but it's easier to say it and feel better about having said it than to actually do anything. 'I showed it at my art show,' she says. 'I hope you don't mind.'

The frame slips slightly in his hands. His fingers don't have feeling right to the tips anymore. Lona asks, 'Do you want me to put it on your bedside table?'

He says, 'Please.'

She clears space between the tissue box and the spare fruit cup and the Inter-Dens and the nail scissors. The woman that Lona never knew smiles. Lona props the two Polaroids on either end. Three generations. Makes it fit.

Grandpa notices the cup of tea Lona made and he stares at it a moment before picking it up, slowly, carefully, and taking a sip. It's not long before he has gulped it down to leafy dregs. The empty cup clatters back into its saucer and he nods, satisfied.

Lona smiles, and crouches down to open her backpack again. 'I also hope you don't mind but I've been borrowing your books.' She gets out *Death on the Nile*, unrecognisable now, AN ART OBJECT emblazoned on its cover. She hands it tentatively to him. 'I did a bunch of these for the show.'

'What is it?' he asks, struggling with the pages. She sees Grandpa's eyes pass uncomprehendingly over the collages and the scrawled pleas to: let me comprehend my own reality. She feels a twinge of shame. She's already sick of her work. It's always the same. Don't do the same thing twice. Make so you don't have to make again.

He looks up and there's a shard of clean black spearing

243

his cloudy irises. 'I'm sorry I couldn't make it,' he says.

Lona thinks of the tampon Monopoly Man and waves a hand, eternally thankful for the opposite. 'Nah, it's all good.'

There's a knock on the door and Grandpa and Lona shout at the same time: 'NO TEA!' The carer is already halfway into the room and jumps a little bit.

'Oh, sorry, yes,' she says, retreating like Russia circa 1915.

Lona says, 'You want me to read you something? *Death on the Nile*?'

Grandpa flicks through the book. 'I'm not sure this is legible.'

Lona pulls another copy out of her bag, filched from the shelf in Ben's old bedroom this morning. 'Don't worry, we've got plenty to spare.'

Call centre

Lona gets a job in a Ticketmaster call centre. She works four days a week and gets sick leave. Her favourite phrase is: you need to speak to Ticketek, we don't sell tickets to the MCG. She enjoys the part where she gets to hang up.

She has a colleague called Rob in the next booth along who has SHORTCAKE inexplicably tattooed on the inside of his arm and she slides effortlessly into inexplicable, debilitating love with him.

She reads spy novels and experimental modernist fiction and true crime on the train to the Hawthorn office.

On Fridays she paints and crochets. She continues to take pictures when people pay her to. She listens to music, binges Netflix, eats snacks and ruins her dinner, gets irritated by her parents, her friends, the world and herself. She messages Tab:

Do you want to see a movie tomorrow?

Tab messages:

u read my mind

The last one

There's a girl up on the platform with her phone plugged into an AUX cord. Planet Skate is reverberating with the sound of 'Cotton Eye Joe.' There is the spongy noise of laughter and the roll of a hundred wheels.

Pat waves from the counter and holds up a hand. The girl leans over the microphone and breaks the bad news: this one's the last one. She's got her pink hair braided across her forehead. She is wearing a black t-shirt over a purple skivvy. Her cheap blue lipstick is faded everywhere but the corners.

Across the room, Lona leans her elbows on the counter and asks Pat, 'Where'd you find the new girl?'

Pat glances over at the pink-haired girl on the stereo platform. 'That's Sissy Nguyen,' she says.

'*That's* Sissy Nguyen?' Lona says, incredulous. Lona went to primary school with Sissy's older sister. Last time she saw Sissy, she was rocking velcro T-bars and a Teenage Mutant Ninja Turtles backpack.

'What are you doing here?' Pat asks.

Lona shrugs. 'Thought I'd just come and say hi.'

'Did you just?' Pat waves at Sissy again. Taps her watch. 'I thought you quit so you'd have weekends off.'

'Yeah, yeah.'

Pat gives her an amused look. 'So you thought you'd just come and say hi, eh?'

Lona wiggles her shoulders up and down, up and down. Her backpack is bulky but light. All she's got in it is her wallet and her skates. 'Yeah, and well...' she says. 'I may as well have a skate while I'm here.'

Floor lights

The big overhead lights go out with a dull clap. Pat leaves the floor lights on. Sissy is sweeping up the chip crumbs and Paddle Pop sticks. She is desperate to get home and changed for a friend's birthday. 'I can finish that up,' Lona tells her.

Sissy says, 'God, you're a gem. Also, who are you?'

Pat heads for the back door with a couple of garbage bags. 'Lona,' she says. 'You planning on staying long?'

'Yeah, I can lock up. I've still got my key.'

'I thought I asked for that back.'

Lona takes the hairy mop from Sissy and sets about sweeping. Pat comes back from the dumpsters and looks around. 'Where's Sissy?'

'I sent her home.'

'*Lona*, you don't work here.' But the Tiges are playing

246

the Demons in the semi-finals and Pat's keen to get home, so she leaves Lona.

Lona gets into her skates, threading up the tired grey laces. She rolls out into the rink. The ground simply slips by underneath her. She's barely touching it, barely any place long enough to make an impact.

It's quiet, dead quiet, and she can hear the friction of her jean legs rubbing against one another: the thst-thst of it. She wonders if Grandpa would've liked to skate, before wheels became a necessary appendage. She wonders if Mum's going to order the lamb curry like she promised. She wonders if she'll run into Rob on the way home. She calculates a two per cent chance considering factors: get a grip, he's just a boy.

She skates backwards, moonwalking. She's got a song stuck in her head and it's not the perfect soundtrack for the moment, in fact it's a really irritating soundtrack for the moment. It's that song that's everywhere right now and maybe that's the only reason that Lona hates it and maybe taste is internalised misogyny like Tab says or maybe it's just a shit song. Who the hell knows.

Lona is skating, and there is a sound like stones being turned over and over in a palm as she circles faster, faster. Her wheels glance across the wounded linoleum that's been bruised by the elbows and knees of a hundred thousand screaming children and her ears are full of blood, heartbeat, viscous juice.

Somewhere, elsewhere, her phone starts to buzz.

Acknowledgements

To everyone at Text, I am so very grateful for your enthusiasm and your belief in *Loner* right from the beginning. I went from no one having read my book to being suddenly overwhelmed by your warmth and passion for all things Lona—you have all made me feel so welcome. To my editor Samantha Forge, I apologise for my tardy email response rate and thank you immensely for your keen insight and your ability to know exactly where my manuscript needed just that little bit more. To Jane Watkins, a hearty thanks for your zeal and your support in my very first attempts to talk publically and articulately about my work. Props to Imogen Stubbs and Rachel Szopa for the zazzy-as-all-heck cover.

Big big love and thanks to ...

Stacey, for the concert and the friendship that made me want to write about concerts and friendship. Kirsti, for always, always, always wanting to talk about books, and also for suffering through the (more horrifying than I intended it to be) horror novel before I let you read this one. Meg, for the many crafty things we have made at your kitchen table, and all the lovely cups of tea and even lovelier chats we have had along the way. Sarah T, for the encouragement from the next bathroom stall along, exactly when I needed help keeping faith. Jess, Lisa, Travis and Cam, for the $5 pasta cups and numerous (oft-aborted) attempts to start a writing group. Y'all are crazy rad.

Thank you to all my lecturers and peers at RMIT, for

the books you recommended and the support you gave and the anthologies we (eventually) named and the reading nights at which some of us drank too much wine and ate too little cheese and were never able to show our face at Captain Melville's again. Particular thanks to Briohny Doyle for her feedback and portentous advice.

Thank you (and apologies) to Tony and Louise for not only giving me my first proper job, but also for unwittingly facilitating the writing of quite a decent portion of this novel behind the counter at Pickwicks.

To be honest, this dedication page should just be one long ode to my parents, not for any specific reason, but for the infinity of their love and support. It occurred to me sometime in the midst of writing this novel that while I used to think the best part of the party was getting to leave and blast the Fratellis in the car, I've come to realise the best part of the party is when I finally get home and kick off my shoes and interrupt your viewing of *Escape to the Country* to give you the run down of exactly which masters degrees and startlingly adult jobs all those people I used to go to school with have now.

To my siblings, for all the absurdities and family folklore we never let each other forget. To my wonderful aunts, uncles and Granma Mac, here's to DIY rolls and big (ten people!!) Christmases.

This book is dedicated to my grandfather. First reader, first fan. You are loved, missed, remembered. Now and always, *salz bitte!*